Panda Books

Chinese Stories from the Fifties

THE years following the founding of the People's Republic in 1949 were significant ones in China's modern political and literary history. Great changes took place in the countryside, in the cities and in personal relationships. *Chinese Stories from the Fifties* is a collection of some of the literature of the period. Some of the stories deal with the setting up of co-operatives and with the period of the Great Leap Forward of 1958, when enthusiasm exceeded reality, others with ethnic minorities or the reconstruction of the country. Many middle-aged and elderly people look back to the successes and failures of the fifties with nostalgia. The youthful idealism that they all shared can be found in these twelve stories.

Chinese Stories
from the Fifties

Panda Books

Panda Books
First edition 1984
Copyright 1984 by CHINESE LITERATURE
ISBN 0-8351-1077-x

Published by CHINESE LITERATURE, Beijing (37), China

Distributed by China International Book Trading Corporation
(GUOJI SHUDIAN), P.O. Box 399, Beijing, China

Printed in the People's Republic of China

CONTENTS

The Election

Qin Zhaoyang

THE people in the village were holding a meeting to discuss whom they should elect in the first nation-wide general election. The population figures entitled them to elect three people's deputies to the *xiang* people's congress. And so far, three candidates had already been agreed upon. The first, Qin Shixue, had been the village Party secretary for six years, the second, Wang Shunde, was a highly respected old traditional medical doctor, and a model medical worker in the county, and the third, Qin Jiagui, a young man in his twenties, was the leader of a model mutual-aid team. But now, it turned out, the women wanted to propose another candidate, no other than Qin Jiagui's wife, Zhang Qiao-feng.

Yin Xiaozhen, a clear-voiced young girl, had the floor. She explained why she wanted to nominate a fourth candidate: "If it hadn't been for Qiaofeng, would her husband have done such a good job on the mutual-aid team? Two years ago, when we had just set it up, we women had never worked in the fields before. Who was it who took the trouble to go to every household and talk the matter over with our parents and in-laws? Who convinced the young women themselves? Later on, who was the first to do the hardest work, and by her example move us so much that we forgot our own aching backs? And then, when it came to assess the amount of work done and portion out the income, who argued for equal pay for equal work, whether done by men or women, and got this adopted at the membership meeting? Last year the women did all the work, from planting to harvesting, in the five *mu* cotton field, so that the men could get on with other work. And we had a record cotton crop, too. Who was it who led us in all this? Dear neighbours, I could just go on and on about Qiaofeng's merits. It is only because she always buries herself in work, and doesn't like to talk, and never brags about herself that some people in our village only know that Qin Jiagui is a model team leader — they have no idea of the things that Qiaofeng has done. . . ."

"I'd like to say something," a young woman called Li Guihua cut in. Pink in the face with excitement, she said, "About a month ago I went to the county model workers' conference as an observer and heard Qin Jiagui report on his model deeds. This is what he said: '*I* called upon the women. *I* talked them into taking part in field work.' He claimed the credit for all that Qiaofeng had done. It came back to all of us at that meeting that he'd said just the same thing at both meetings of our *xiang* model workers. And when I came back and talked it over with our chairman of the women's association here, I heard then that the village leaders had already criticized him for this very thing. He admitted he was wrong then, but when he got to the county he forgot all about Qiaofeng just the same, and only remembered about himself. I *must* bring this up today. We can't let Qiaofeng's merits remain unknown!" She cast a glance at Qin Jiagui, tossed back her braids and sat down.

A sudden silence descended upon the meeting and all eyes turned to Qin Jiagui.

If he had stood up at this moment, said something nice about his wife Qiaofeng, and admitted his own shortcomings, he could yet have won the day. But he didn't. He was so used to enjoying the honours. He knew beforehand that the people would pick him as a candidate and would almost certainly ask him to make a speech. In fact he had put on his new blue cotton suit specially for the occasion. Now, with all eyes on him, this new suit made him more embarrassed than ever and he didn't know which way to turn. He stole a glance at Qiaofeng sitting by his side, and wished to goodness she would say something. Now, if only she'd say something like this — "Fellow villagers, don't blame Jiagui unduly . . . after all, I owe what progress I've made so far entirely to his help." But Qiaofeng remained silent, with her head down and her hair nearly screening her face. She had never spoken at a full meeting yet.

"Fellow villagers!" Qin Jiagui simply had to get up on his feet. He felt dry in the mouth, and his voice was husky. "What Li Guihua said just now is not true. . . ."

"It is!" Li Guihua interrupted loudly. "I fully admit you're a good mutual-aid team leader and you have done a lot to push forward production in our village; I approve of you as a candidate as well. But today's meeting is so very important. I simply *must* speak about

Qiaofeng's good points and that makes me mention your shortcomings. I must tell the truth."

"I fully agree with Guihua." Wang Guiyong, the chairman of the women's association put in. "This is a meeting for the election. We must exercise our rights as citizens properly. We shouldn't leave Zhang Qiaofeng out. And I must say Comrade Jiagui *is* rather vain and he does love to brag about himself."

Silence fell. Only a few old people in the back rows whispered to one another: "These young women are taking it too seriously. It's so embarrassing for Jiagui. After all, the two are man and wife. What does it matter which one is elected?"

The chairman put the proposal to the vote. Raising their hands and cheering, the people unanimously accepted Zhang Qiaofeng as a fourth candidate.

Qin Jiagui never dreamt that people thought so highly of his wife. At first he was just astonished; then he got angry and bitter; he was particularly annoyed with the women in his team. "Well!" he thought to himself indignantly. "You made some progress, but it was I who led you forward. Now you turn around and criticize me like this. You've no sense of decency!" He wanted to leave the meeting straight away. . . . He had no ears for the Party secretary's speech, nor did he hear the people ask Wang Shunde, the old doctor, to speak. It was only when the chairman had twice called on him by name that he came out of his trance.

He pulled himself together, cleared his throat and walked to the rostrum. Even now, if he seized the opportunity to criticize himself and asked the people to elect Qiaofeng instead of himself, then the electors would certainly have thought well of him. What a pity that he again missed his chance and only tried to win back his prestige by an impressive speech. . . .

"Dear neighbours, my mutual-aid team was the first one in this village. . . ." He repeated once again the old, old story. He began two years back, went on to last year, and then brought them up to the present. It was a long-winded speech, without an atom of anything new in it.

"The same old story again, showing off as usual," one of the villagers whispered.

"No need to go on chanting psalms about your model deeds — we know them by heart already," said another.

Qin Jiagui was oblivious of the whisperers, and went on and on. At long last his speech wound to a close. And then deafening applause broke out, but it was not him, not for Qin Jiagui and his long speech. It was for Zhang Qiaofeng, whom the chairman called on to say a few words. Cries for Qiaofeng mingled with the clapping of hands.

Tugging and pulling, the women finally succeeded in getting Qiaofeng to go to the platform. Qin Jiagui saw her suddenly lift her head, pull her shoulders back and stand up straight. Her rosy cheeks glowed and her great black eyes sparkled. She even seemed taller than usual. She tossed back a lock of hair from her forehead and, to his astonishment, started to speak quite composedly.

"Dear neighbours, today, when I look back, I feel a bit uneasy. First of all, during the busy harvest time this year, I had intended to organize the team members and set up a seasonal nursery, to free the mothers with small children for work in the fields. But then, because I was a bit under the weather and because I thought it would be difficult, I didn't manage to get it done. I blame myself for lacking a resolute enough will to overcome difficulties. Secondly, although it's almost three years since our mutual-aid team was founded, it still hasn't become a co-operative. This also shows that I haven't done enough in working for it. . . . No matter whether I'm elected or not, I'm going to work for these two things."

She said the last sentence with particular emphasis. Another round of thunderous applause burst out.

"Look at our Qiaofeng, who only looks forward; *she* doesn't only talk of what has already been done!" cried the straightforward Li Guihua, running over to hug Qiaofeng, laughing until she had to stop for breath.

All at once, Qiaofeng's mother-in-law stood up. Gesticulating with her hands, she fairly moaned out: "But this is terrible! We've only got three deputies for our *xiang* and now you've put up four candidates. Of course everyone will want to vote for the Party secretary, and who wouldn't vote for our respected old Mr Wang Shunde? And now, that leaves only two, my son and my daughter-in-law. Which one shall we elect?"

It was clear what she meant. If her daughter-in-law were elected, her son would be deeply upset; she knew this all too well. And she was not the only one to realize it either. But the chairman had already announced that the meeting was adjourned, and no one felt like troubling his head over such a small detail as this. After all, it was an election, wasn't it? One must be impartial, and elect whoever was really good, regardless of whether it was a man or a woman.

Qin Jiagui strode off. When he got home he threw

himself down on the *kang* without a word. A few minutes later he heard Qiaofeng chattering happily with his mother in the kitchen, as she gave a hand with the cooking.

"Well, you...." He gnashed his teeth.

"Qiaofeng, come here," he suddenly bawled out.

Qiaofeng came in, her hands covered with flour, and her face beaming.

"What ever do you think you were talking about in the meeting?"

"Why, what did I say?" Qiaofeng was startled.

"Why did you have to say all that in the meeting today? You even said that our team hasn't become a co-op in three years. What did you mean by saying that?"

"Oh! So that's the kind of person you are!" Qiaofeng, who was honest and gentle by nature, could not help getting angry.

Of course, one thing led to another; they quarrelled. Both of them were too upset to eat.

So was the old lady. She could not say her daughter-in-law was in the wrong, nor did she have the heart to reproach her son. Wringing her hands and stamping her feet in despair, she sighed and groaned. Finally she could no longer bear it alone. She trotted off to find somebody to pour out her troubles to without thinking about the outcome.

First she got hold of the chairman of the women's association: "My dear chairman, didn't I tell you you shouldn't have both of them as candidates? All the time they've been married, they've never quarrelled like this; they didn't even want to eat...." Then on she went to Li Guihua and poured out the whole story to her, in great detail.

Both Wang Cuiyong and Li Guihua became angry. Then there was Yin Xiaozhen, who lived next door to the Qins. Of course she had overheard everything, especially all that was said by Qin Jiagui when he raised his voice. In no time all the women and quite a few of the men of the village were indignantly saying what they thought of Qin Jiagui.

In the evening, the meeting to elect the deputies was held. The result was a great surprise to them all, even those who had half expected some such outcome. Qin Jiagui only got three votes, while practically everyone voted for Zhang Qiaofeng.

This was too heavy a blow for Qin Jiagui to bear. He left before the meeting was over, and his mother followed him, wailing.... When Wang Cuiyong and Qin Shixue arrived later with Qiaofeng, there he was lying motionless on the *kang,* his head buried under the quilt. He would not answer a word when they spoke to him, feeling like an outcast of the people. His mother, who had obviously failed to cheer him up, had already gone to bed; she could be heard tossing and muttering on the *kang* in her room.

As Jiagui persisted in silence, Qiaofeng sent the Party secretary and the chairman of the women's association home; she would talk to him herself. When they were alone she folded back the quilt from Jiagui's face and saw that there were even hot tears in his eyes. She kissed him on the cheek, and said tenderly: "I'm not angry with you, you old silly, but really you should think about it...."

"Yes, Qiaofeng, I know I should think it over. . . ." he said in a choked voice, while a tear trickled down from the corner of his eye.

Translated by Zhang Suchu

Qin Zhaoyang was born in 1916 in Huanggang County, Hubei Province. After Liberation, he was appointed assistant editor of the monthly People's Literature *and an executive member of the editorial board of* The Literary Gazette. *His chief works are the story collections* On the Plain *and* Happiness, *the novel* Advance Across the Fields *and the prize-winning children's story* Adventures of a Little Swallow. *He is now deputy director of the People's Literature Publishing House in Beijing.*

My Young Friend

Du Pengcheng

ONE morning last autumn I stood by the highway hoping to get a lift to Longting, south of Mount Qinling, where I had to attend a conference. But all the cars which passed were fully loaded; there seemed to be no possible chance of a lift. I looked anxiously at my watch and realized that if I wanted to get there on time I must hurry — I had nearly 30 kilometres to cover. Finally, in desperation, I went back to the engineering section, a unit of the Baoji-Chengdu Railway Construction Administration, to ask the Party secretary there for a car. I felt I must get to the conference on time.

The Party secretary was most co-operative. "That's all right — we'll get you there!" he said. "The sedan's out but one of the lorries can take you down." He stroked his chin as he calculated the distance and then said, "If you're pressed for time, get Wang Chun to drive you. You don't know him? Ah, that's your loss. He's quite a character here; fine chap in every way but a little bit too light-hearted."

I followed the Party secretary to the transport corps' park. We stopped by a lorry under which someone was hammering and knocking away, with only his legs visible.

"That you, Young Wang? Take a comrade to Long-ting, will you?"

Wang Chun scrambled out from under the lorry, turned a crisp somersault before our eyes like a professional acrobat and landed lightly on his feet. Only then did he see that there was a stranger there, and hurriedly assumed a serious look. He was not tall, and his heavy working clothes, his khaki trousers, the kind worn by the Chinese People's Volunteers in Korea, and his maroon leather jacket and boots did not add to his height. A greasy worker's cap sat jauntily over one eye and a white towel was wrapped tightly round his thick neck. He gave the impression of being made of muscle only, taut muscle. He pulled off his dirty old gloves, thrust them into one pocket, and said "Hop in" with a jerk of his head. He had rather a hoarse voice.

As he started the car I had a chance to look him over. There were a few small scars behind his right ear and on his forehead, which might be relics of boyhood scraps, or from a wound received in Korea. His mouth looked determined, but the downy growth on his face betrayed the fact that he was still only a lad.

As soon as he left the car park we gathered speed and flew as if on wings up the winding mountain track. Young Wang steered the car with a firm hand, his head erect, his lips compressed and his big round eyes looking straight ahead. He reminded me of an athlete in a hundred-metre sprint. The lorry raced uphill and then down. The steep cliff-like cuttings rose beside us, now on the right, now on the left, but we never slowed down: the twists and turns made me quite dizzy. This young man with his surplus energy seemed determined to send me down a ten-thousand-foot precipice, it seemed! To do him justice, though, he was really an extremely good driver and we flew along quite smoothly. I almost felt as though I were riding in a speed-boat over rippling waves.

When we had reached the summit of Mount Qinling I looked back. The sight fairly took my breath away. The road we had come up looked no wider than a metre or so, lying up the hillsides like a strip of ribbon. I was again impressed by Young Wang's driving when I remembered how fast we had moved, and what a height we had reached, seemingly so effortlessly. We had started in the foot-hills, where my light jacket was quite enough, but already, when we were only halfway up the hill it had begun to get chilly. Then we went through the clouds which girdled the mountain, and now, on the top, the snow was falling. It blew hard on the windshield, and when it was wiped off the glare from the snow all round made you blink.

Wang Chun halted and jumped down to have a look at the engine. He seemed to have springs on his feet, the way he hopped off and on, like an acrobat diving through fire-rings. He slammed the door briskly, settled down on his seat and poked his head out of the window. Then, with a loud starter's whistle, he shouted, "Forward at a speed of 40 kilometres per hour!" and we were off again.

We got to a little town where the peasants were out with cymbals and drums — I learned later that they were celebrating joining an agricultural co-op. I wanted a drink of water, and asked Wang to stop for a few minutes, thinking he too would welcome the chance to stretch his legs. In fact, from what I had seen of him

I expected him to be out in a flash, but no. He only gave a casual glance at the cheering crowd, pulled the towel off his neck and wiped his hands, and then produced an exercise book and a textbook from under his seat. These he opened and began work. I looked at the subject. He was doing some algebra problems.

We must have been there about ten minutes when another lorry pulled up behind us. A young fellow got out from beside the driver. He too mopped his brows with a towel. He glared at us and said, "Hey, you over there! Who do you think you are, shouting and cursing the way you did when you wanted to overtake us back there."

I was so startled that I nearly spilled my bowl of water. That young man was certainly asking for trouble I thought, provoking a tiger like our Young Wang! I expected him to rush out and join battle, but he didn't stir, and went on with his exercises without a word.

Just then, the driver got down from the newly arrived lorry. He was an old chap, and went slowly round his own vehicle, his hands behind his back, examining it carefully, and kicking each tyre. He glanced at the celebrating crowd nearby. I had recognized him by now — it was Chang, who had taken me to town for a meeting a few days ago.

"Hello, Comrade Chang! Nice to see you again," I said.

Chang gave me a brief nod and came up to our lorry. He stood by us without a word, and looked at Wang Chun. To my great surprise Wang Chun scrambled out of his seat at once, apparently drawn by the eagle gaze of those old eyes.

"Good-day, Uncle Chang. I haven't seen you for

some weeks," he said, standing respectfully before the older man. His face was red as fire, and he doodled nervously on the hood with one hand.

I didn't know at the time, but I found out afterwards what their relationship was. Wang Chun, I found, had lost his mother when he was still a baby and was brought up by his father, a machinist. His father died before Wang Chun was grown-up, worn out by thirty years' toil for rapacious factory owners. He left nothing on his death, not even a thin mat to be buried in. Old Chang and Wang's father were old workmates and friends, they had often shared a drop of wine and drowned the sorrows of poverty together. Old Chang bought a mat and arranged for the burial of his friend, and Old Chang took upon himself the task of bringing up the only one left in this poor worker's family. Not long afterwards, Old Chang lost his factory job and started long-distance lorry driving for private merchants. He used to take Wang Chun with him on the road. Old Chang would toss his bedding roll into the cabin and then put Wang Chun on the seat by his side saying, "Watch the luggage, boy." Wang would snuggle up against the bedding and doze off in the rocking, bumpy vehicle. This went on for two years; a rough life. They sometimes slept in the lorry, sometimes in little inns and sometimes out in the wild. Then the People's Liberation Army liberated Tianjin and Old Chang, with a group of other workers, went south to repair the railway during the People's War of Liberation. Before he left, he arranged for Wang Chun to go into a machine shop as odd-job boy. His parting words were, "All his life, your father worked on machines, but he wasn't even able to buy himself a coffin for a decent burial. The workers have become the masters of the country now. Mind you do your best at work." In 1951, Old Chang joined a workers' volunteer brigade in the Korean War. He was back on lorry driving, and who should his assistant turn out to be? None other than Wang Chun, now eighteen. These two, far closer than ordinary master and apprentice, shared hardships and troubles and worked as one on the Korean transport line.

All this I found out afterwards. All I saw now was Old Chang prowling round Wang Chun's lorry with a highly critical eye and an inquiring hand. He gave it an expert going over, in fact. When he had finished he seemed fairly well satisfied with the maintenance work of his former apprentice. He knew the lorry well: It was the same lorry they had been on together in Korea, but now the shrapnel scratches were hardly noticeable.

Finally he looked pointedly at the "Good Driver" badge on the fender. "H'm," he said. " 'Safely driven for 100,000 kilometres,' eh? I suppose you're a skilled driver now."

Young Wang swallowed; you'd think there was a sour plum in his mouth. "Come off it," he said awkwardly. "You should know whether or not I'm any good."

"People who bawl out the driver they want to overtake, the way you did, must reckon themselves top-rate drivers." Old Chang's tone was very dry.

Wang's cheek muscles twitched, and I could see the sweat break out on his forehead. "Well ... I ...." was all he could get out.

Old Chang looked over and through him. There was a pause. Then he spoke again. "I hear you've been given a citation." Young Wang's eyelids fluttered wildly. I had the feeling he would have given anything to escape from this interview.

I tried to say something to ease the situation, "He told me on the road that he had one citation for good work and one reprimand, and that he thought the two just balance out. I rather liked that way of putting it, myself."

All I got for this was a glare from Young Wang. Apparently he felt it was no help to get this wisecrack repeated at this juncture.

Old Chang ignored me as he had Wang. "There's plenty of good stuff in you," he said gruffly, stomping back to his own lorry. "Pity you don't let it out the best way." As he opened the door he threw another remark over his shoulder, "I ran into Young Fan the other day and he told me you've found yourself a girl."

Wang went scarlet again. "Aw, take no notice of his gabbing. Who d'you think would love a man with a head like mine?"

On our way back, quite late, we found more than a foot of snow up on Mount Qinling. We ploughed through it, throwing up a white wave on each side. Suddenly there was a loud knocking and we stopped with a jerk. What a rotten place to break down in! I followed Young Wang down and together we tried what a bit of pushing would do, but it was no use. Young Wang waved me aside, brushed a patch of road clear of snow and crawled under the chassis. After what seemed a long time he located the trouble and did something. He wriggled awkwardly out and said we should be all right now, but when it came to him getting back again into the cab, he couldn't do it. His trousers were frozen solid and he couldn't bend his legs. It took quite a bit of banging at them before he could get in and start up.

It was three a.m. when we got back and I thought that even Young Wang's surplus energy must be pretty well used up from such a gruelling day. Not a bit of it! He fussed around his precious lorry, draining the radiator, brushing the cabin and even wiping down windows. I paced up and down to keep my feet warm.

"Why don't you go home to bed?" asked Wang.

"I can't get over to my bunk at this hour," I said. "I'll stick round here a bit until it's light."

Young Wang took me to the drivers' hut. There was a communal bunk there, with three men rolled up asleep on it and a nice warm stove. Young Wang showed me where his bedding was and said I could sleep there and then went out. But I was too wet and cold to sleep. I tried to warm up by the stove, but then realized I had to go out. It was still completely dark outside, except for a few twinkling lights on the surrounding hills where the work went on unceasingly. As I looked around I saw the light go on in a hut nearby. Young Wang was standing by a window, and I could hear his loud whisper, "Li Yiyong! Little Li!"

"Who's that?" came a girl's voice. "What on earth does anybody want at this time of night?"

"It's me," said Young Wang, rather subdued. "I want Little Li."

"Is that so! And what do you want Li Yiyong for, may I ask?"

"I've got something I want to discuss with her," said Wang hopefully.

"For goodness' sake! What a time to choose, waking

everyone up too.   Li Yiyong's not here anyway, she's on the night shift.   If you really want to see her you'll have to climb up the hill."

"I know that's you, Little Zhao," said Wang, coaxingly.   "You're not really cross with me, are you?   It might have been someone coming to see you, you know. I bet you wouldn't mind that!"

"Oh, go away! You're breaking the rules of the hostel and I'll see that you catch it tomorrow," was the stern answer.

Young Wang turned back, and bumped into me. "Oh you!" he said, rather embarrassed.   "Thought you'd be in bed by now." I wasn't going to be put off like that.   "Well, I'm not," I said.   "What's all this with you and Li Yiyong, and who's the young lady behind the windows?"

"Don't talk so loud," he said hastily as we walked back to the drivers' hut.   "Li Yiyong is my girl.   She works on an air compressor. That scissor tongue you heard is Zhao. . . . She's on the switchboard. She's only a kid really, but can she talk! When I first got friendly with Li Yiyong, she used to help me and carry messages to her, but since that wretched business last Wednesday, she's changed.   Anyone would think she'd swallowed a fly the way she looks when she sees me!"

What had happened last Wednesday? Apparently Young Wang had returned from a trip at midnight with a lovely red Korean apple.   He was set on giving it to Little Li at once, but he was a bit baffled to know how, feeling he couldn't very well wake her up at midnight. But it nearly burned a hole in his pocket, the way he wanted to give it to her.   Of course it wasn't only the chance of giving her an apple that was on his mind.

After all, he'd not seen her for three whole days! In the end he told himself that even if she wouldn't be keen on an apple, at least it was an excuse to see her and hold her hand for a minute, or at least hear her voice. So off he went to her window, and whispered her name. It was his bad luck that the job was at a most critical stage, and an emulation campaign was on. The air compressors had been running all out and Little Li was dead to the world as soon as she closed her eyes. If the sky fell she wouldn't have woken — it was a waste of breath whispering. But Wang's hopeful nature wasn't easily daunted. He knew which was her bed and thought he'd just toss the apple on to it through the window. It never crossed his mind that he wouldn't aim straight, much less that it would fall squarely on Little Zhao's nose. She screamed and woke them all up. What a to-do! Five startled girls putting on the lights and yelling their heads off. Wang made off quick, and they didn't know what had happened. When the security comrades came the next day to investigate they found the apple and traced it back to Young Wang.

The story was too good to be kept to a small circle and it went round the whole site. Poor Wang came in for a lot of teasing.

I was amused about it myself, and wanted to know what the cause of this trouble was like. Was she like that chubby girl at the co-op sales-counter? Or perhaps like that garrulous young thing in the Youth League office? Maybe she looked like that student-engineer fresh from college.

Wang was more than willing to tell me all about her. Like so many of our youngsters today, Li Yiyong had come to the construction site in search of the ideal job by which she could carry out her youthful dreams of serving the country. She had arrived from the south about a year ago, and straight away started giving the comrades in charge of personnel a real headache. They suggested she should train as an accountant but she claimed that she was in mortal fear of figures; they asked her to be a telephone operator, but she protested that there was no technique to be learned in that. What did she want to do then, they asked. That, she couldn't quite say except that it had to be a job where she could acquire technical knowledge. One of the men in charge of personnel, busy as he was, spent long hours reasoning with her, but she was quite determined. Finally he said, "All right, I'll send you to the engineering section and let the chief there find suitable work for you." That brought Li Yiyong to this section.

But that still didn't mean she had the job she wanted. The chief's first suggestion was the switchboard! Li Yiyong was very scornful and asked if that was the only job on the whole construction site. Technical knowledge was her demand; she made the further suggestion that she would like to work on the air compressors. That was asking too much, really wilful, so the local Youth League organization officer was asked to speak to her. That was none other than Wang Chun. As a matter of fact, they decided to send her to work on the air compressors in the end, but only after criticizing her for picking and choosing work in an individualistic way. Wang Chun had to talk to her about it again and again, and somehow both of them began to feel there was something amiss unless they saw each other every day. But Wang, as a driver, had to be out all day and half the night, so it was not possible for them to be together too much. That only seemed to make their hearts grow fonder.

Wang gave me only an outline of this, of course, as he changed his wet clothes. "Do get to bed," he said, kicking his dirty clothes under the bed. "I can get my sleep during the day. I think I'll go up the hill now and have a word with her." He cocked his head and appeared to be listening. "You know," he confided. "I can pick out her machine anywhere."

I felt a bit like trying to dissuade him. It seemed a daft thing to go up that rough hillside in the dark, and he must be pretty tired, but from what I knew of him I realized it would be a waste of breath. I don't suppose he gave a thought to being cold or tired, with love burning so strongly in his breast!

It was early morning when I got back to the hostel, thinking to get a bit of sleep. But before I could do this I heard there was to be a big blasting operation and hurried over to see it. It must have been three or so in the afternoon, while I was still on the site and the operation was over, when I heard that there had been a bad landslide and that several lorries had been buried on the road, with maybe over fifty people involved. Someone said Wang Chun was the driver of one of the lorries. The news hit me like a blow. Wang Chun, so full of life, buried under a mass of falling earth? It could not be!

I rushed over to the engineering section to find the Party secretary. If Wang Chun was really swallowed up by the mountain I must help the other comrades to dig him out, I felt.

The Party secretary was pacing back and forth in his

office, greatly agitated. One of the clerks was on the telephone.

"Who is it? The bureau office? Yes, yes, this is the Party committee at the engineering section. No, we don't know the exact situation yet. . . ." As soon as he replaced the receiver the telephone rang again. This time it was a work-team calling to ask whether any of the lorries or people involved came from their team. No sooner had they rung off than someone else wanted to know how soon the road would be cleared as there was an important load to go up the mountain in two hours' time. The clerk finally put down the receiver. "This is dreadful," he exclaimed. "Thousands of square metres of earthwork have collapsed."

The Party secretary looked first at me and then at the clerk but he said not a word.

I looked on the map for the place where the landslide occurred. I had heard something about this particular area from the local people when I first came, I remembered. We were talking about landslides and someone said that during the Three Kingdoms period in the third century a battalion of Cao Cao's men had been swallowed up by the mountains. Evidently landslides had occurred round these parts from early days.

I decided I would go to the fall with the Party secretary, but we hadn't got out of the office when a young girl entered. She was in grease-stained overalls and her face was pale. She looked at the Party secretary with eyes that seemed to have lost their lustre and tried to speak, but words failed her and she stood miserably by the wall.

The gloom on the Party secretary's face suddenly lifted; he brightened visibly and seemed relaxed and cheerful. "Hello there, Little Li," he said, "I suppose you've come for news about Wang Chun. You'll have to keep calm. I've sent someone down to see what's happened. Like you, I don't believe anything can happen to him. You know how nippy he is on his feet! Remember the way he never got caught by bombs in Korea? He must have dodged them at least a dozen times."

This was Li Yiyong, I realized, Wang Chun's beloved.

She wasn't comforted by the secretary's word but turned her face away and began to sob convulsively.

"Come now, little one," he said, gently. "Don't cry! There's no definite news yet — nothing's verified. We're going there now. D'you want to come with us?"

"No," said Li between sobs. "I . . . I can't."

I had no words to console the poor girl with and left the office with a heavy heart. I grabbed a bicycle and raced down the highway along the river bank, but I had not gone far before I ran into a solid block of waiting lorries, horse carts, pack mules, donkeys, barrows and countless people. The line seemed to be interminable.

When I got to the scene of the accident, dust was still swirling about, as though after a large-scale explosion. The nearby temporary huts had been badly shaken. It looked, in fact, as though there'd been an earthquake. I could see across the great fall now; where the road emerged again at the other side was also packed with people, vehicles and animals.

Work had already started on making a provisional road. Standing near, in earnest discussion, was a group of people. I recognized among them the director of the

Engineering Bureau and his deputy, and the chief engineer.

I went over to them and saw at once, when the director turned in my direction, that the accident was not as bad as we had feared. Six lorries were involved, he told me, but all the passengers were saved. It must have been a close shave! But his last sentence worried me. "I only hope Wang Chun's injuries are not too serious. . . ."

Of course I wanted to know more, but I felt I couldn't ask any more questions. The director had more than enough worries as it was. I went on and found someone who could tell me what had happened.

This road across Mount Qinling is a very important one. It is one of the main arteries in the building of the Baoji-Chengdu Railway. Any hold-up on it, or break-down, would cause a traffic block kilometres long at once. Yesterday's explosion, therefore, had been recognized as likely to cause trouble. It was a big blast, which cut a large outcrop in two. Masses of rocks and earth had fallen near and partly on to the road itself, and squads of workers were standing by to keep the road clear and the traffic moving. There was a lookout posted as well for landslides — temperamental behaviour was to be expected from Mount Qinling. Then, some time before noon the lookout, as he stood vigilantly with a red flag in his hands and a whistle between his lips, saw some young trees on a hillside above the road were shaking. He thought it might be caused by breeze and tossed a handful of dust across. It settled quietly — no sign of wind. He looked at a distant hilltop: there the smoke rose straight up. No, there was no wind! "That's funny," he mused. "There's not a bit of wind but the trees are swaying. What is it, a landslide?" Just at that moment he saw six lorries coming down the road, right underneath this threatening hill. He blew his whistle frantically, waved his warning flag, and did everything he could to attract the drivers' attention. But they were on the danger spot already. Their only escape now was to accelerate and get out of danger by going through it! This they tried, but even as they shot forward rocks began to rain down. One as large as a house landed right in front of the leading lorry — Wang Chun's lorry, as I learned later. He looked round to see if he could reverse and go back. . . too late, the fall was too near and too fast. He was an experienced hand at these falls, and knew he could escape by running. But to his horror he saw that the lorries behind him carried a mixed bag of passengers, who panicked.

Wang Chun ran towards them, waving frantically. "Run north," he shouted. "Up there! Run north."

Unfortunately most of the passengers were new to this area and had no idea what to do. Some of them were peasants from nearby villages who had come as temporary labourers to the site, and some were wives or mothers coming to see their families. They ran round helplessly, not knowing how to get to safety. Some dived under the lorries, and some even ran in the worst direction, straight towards the crumbling hill. One woman got out of the danger zone by chance, and then ran back to the crowd by the lorries. Wang Chun and the other drivers set out to save the bewildered passengers, fifty-two of them, running after them one by one and pointing out the safest place. Some had to be dragged out from underneath and pushed into running for their lives. Finally everyone was safe, or so they thought, and the drivers then made for safety themselves. Wang Chun was just turning to go when a little old woman suddenly came out from behind the third lorry, clasping a bundle and peering round with frightened eyes. She was paralysed with fear. Wang Chun danced in his anxiety. He turned back to rescue her, and the sentry yelled at him and waved. The landslide was well under way now. Stones and earth were coming down thicker than ever and a narrow black crack had opened ominously on the hillside above. A whole side of the mountain was going to fall at any moment. One of the other drivers turned back, but Wang Chun halted him. Despite the sentry's wild signals, and despite his own knowledge of the danger, Wang knew he must try and save her. "Keep away! No good two of us risking it," he shouted to the other driver, and dashed back to the road. He grabbed hold of her arm and rushed for safety. They nearly made it; there were only two yards or so to go when Wang Chun saw the whole mass moving on to them and felt the gush of air. There would not be time! With a final desperate effort, he shoved the old woman forward with all his strength. She fell over and crawled to safety, but Wang Chun fell. The mountain of earth crashed down in a tremendous burst right over him.

Thousands of workers, from the nearby units without waiting for orders rushed over to help in the rescue work. They didn't hesitate but started working at once over the whole fall, even on the part where further slides might occur.

The lookout had marked where Wang Chun was buried — it was at the edge of the fall — and directed the workers to dig there at once. They got to him quite quickly. His nose and eyes were full of earth, and there was blood on his lips. A doctor hurried up, gave him first aid and rushed him off to the hospital in an ambulance, its siren screaming.

The doctor was inundated with anxious inquiries but he could not say more than that all he could see, from a quick examination, was that there were very few external signs of injury. Whether there was serious internal damage, and whether his life was in danger would have to be seen in hospital.

For three days the hospital wouldn't let anyone visit Wang Chun. On the fourth day I got permission to go. When I arrived the Party secretary of the engineering section was already there.

Wang Chun told us briefly what had happened, and what he had felt like. Then he turned to the Party secretary with a face full of woe. "I hear you've given me a citation! Fat lot of good that is to anyone! My lorry's been crushed, the lorry I drove in Korea! It's part of me, I can't be without it."

While we were talking we heard a girl's voice. She sounded impatient. Almost immediately Little Li came in, all smartened up with a fresh ribbon in her hair. She stood still in the doorway for a minute. Her eyes shot on to Wang Chun's face, and her lips broke into a loving, mischievous smile. Then she saw me and the Party secretary and bit it back. "Wang Chun," she said, in mock seriousness. "I hear you're trying to get discharged from hospital as soon as you can! Have you had enough of living, stupid?"

Wang Chun chuckled and energetically waved his

arms. "There's nothing the matter with me, really," he said. "I'll get up and show you if you like!"

"Hey, none of that," I said. "Don't go showing off, now."

Little Li looked round the room as casually as she could. It seemed as if she'd always been sure that nothing could happen to him. She tried to keep up this facade. "It would have been all right even if you'd lost your life," she said. "Between you, you drivers managed to save more than fifty lives!"

"Oho!" said the Party secretary. "So that's how she feels, is it, Wang Chun? D'you hear that? That came from the bottom of her heart."

Little Li couldn't keep back a giggle. She flashed a look sideways at Wang Chun to see how he was taking it. Then her face changed. "Do you know who the old woman you saved was?" she asked.

"What do you think!" said Wang scornfully. "D'you expect me to wait for an introduction at a time like that? Really, Little Li, you look quite intelligent, but it's obviously all surface. Pity that such a pretty head should have nothing behind it."

Little Li smiled at him. "It was my mother," she said. "She was coming to see me. Now she owes you her life."

Young Wang's hand came down on the bed with a bang. "Gosh! What a way to meet your future mother-in-law for the first time. Just my luck! All she knows of me is that I gave her such a shove."

Little Li blushed red as fire. "Mother-in-law!" she said indignantly. "You flatter yourself, don't you?" She stifled another giggle. "I agree you are too rough, though. You gave mum a terrible push! She fell down and scratched her hands and knees badly, but all you do is brag about it."

"I think we'd better go," said the Party secretary with a grin. "I somehow feel we're in the way here."

May 1956

Translated by Jia Ding

Du Pengcheng was born in Han-cheng County, Shaanxi Province in 1921. A war correspondent before Liberation, he joined Xinhua News Agency in 1951. Since 1954 he has published the novel Defend Yan'an, *the novella* In Days of Peace *and the anthologies* The Immortal City *and* Young Friends. *He is vice-chairman of the Xi'an branch of the Chinese Writers' Association.*

Around the Spring Festival

Wang Wenshi

THE Spring Festival holidays were just over. There was still an air of festivity over the village, but after breakfast, when the sun was bright and the day warm, the peasants were back at work. The men had started carting manure to the co-op fields while the women stayed at home spinning and weaving, preparing summer clothes for their families. Wheels rolled, looms hummed. Everywhere was a cheerful bustle.

But this did not apply to Dajie of Nanzhao Village. If you had told people that Dajie had no appetite for work but was boiling with indignation, no one would have believed you. The sun had alighted on the window-sills, but she had not yet prepared breakfast; the bed was not made, nor the floor swept. She was standing in the courtyard shouting at the dog and shooing the hens. Then picking up a stick, she started chasing all over the place after the piglets that had broken loose from the sty. When she had quelled the hens, dog and piglets, she stood in the middle of the courtyard, feeling at a loose end and thoroughly bored.

She cast an indifferent glance at the outer gate, which was bolted and locked. The latches and lock were performing their duty well, shutting out everything, even the awakening spring, which could now only quietly climb the white poplar and peep in. In the yard, all was topsy-turvy: the neat stacks of hay and firewood had been scattered all over the place by the chickens and pigs.

Dajie lowered her head. Suddenly she realized that the stick she was holding in her hand was the one used for mixing the cattle feed. As if it were unlucky or had burned her hands, she wrinkled her nose in distaste, looked at the wall to the north and, with all her might, sent the stick hurtling through the air over the wall.

In the room, the child was wailing. She stepped in and snapped at it, "Cry, cry yourself dead and stop plaguing me! Once you're all dead I'll have some peace!" After giving vent to her feelings, she sank listlessly on to the *kang*. Then, her heart softened by the child's cries, she reached out and hugged him closely to her breast.

The cheerful bustle in the village lanes made itself heard from time to time over the wall. People's voices, the cracking of whips and the rumbling of wheels intermingled with the sounds of the pedlars' rattles and the cries of the old beancurd seller. Occasionally the mobile stall vendor from the consumers' co-operative could be heard shouting through a megaphone, "Neighbours — crystal sugar, sweets, matches, kerosene, tea...." Trailing behind the medley of sounds were the merry shouts of swarms of children scurrying about. How tempting all this was! Dajie looked at the lamp and thought, "It's time to get it filled. The sugar is running short too." She lifted one corner of the mat on the *kang*, took out a wad of brand-new banknotes, stood there irresolutely a little while, then suddenly heaved a deep sigh and stuffed the money back under the pillow. Taking the child in her arms, she sat there stiffly, motionless as a statue.

A resonant bass voice broke in on her reverie, making her raise her head to listen intently. The voice said, "Give me that whip." Then again, "Yu, yu, yu!" — the call for the beast to halt. Then, sharp cracks of the whip and the man's roar: "Da, da, huo . . . huo . . . da, da, huo . . . huo . . . huo . . . yu! . . . See? That's the way to handle it. The way you tried to force him uphill just won't do. You should have more concern for our cattle, old man! What if you kill one? You'll pay for it, eh? Ha . . . ha."

Dajie was trying all the while to detect some trace of sorrow and loneliness in the voice, to find some crumb of comfort for herself. But no, there was nothing. In exasperation she told the child who was too small to understand, "Little Doggie, that ungrateful father of yours has abandoned us both. He's washed his hands of us!" She decided to turn a deaf ear to the goings-on outside. But that proved impossible. Her man's voice, so sweet yet painful to her ears, was tugging at her heart-strings. It was coming closer too. He seemed to have stopped at their gate.

"He's coming back!" she thought. For a second she didn't know what to do. Then she hastily put down the child, snatched up a cloth and wiped the top of the cooking-range and the table. Then she combed her hair, and looked into the mirror.

Bang, bang, bang! Someone was knocking at the gate.

"I shouldn't have shut the gate. How can I possibly go and open it for him?" she thought regretfully. Then

again, "Well, maybe it's not such a bad thing after all!
Let him just walk in as he pleases? Oh no, that's making it far too easy for him."

Bang, bang, bang!

Dajie ignored the knocking, and went on tidying up
the room.

Bang, bang, bang!

Mirror in hand, lips pursed, she gave a contented
little laugh and murmured to herself, "Go on, go on
knocking. You'll have to keep it up till all the neighbours have heard, I'll see to that!"

Bang, bang, bang!

"Dajie, open the gate!" It was the voice of an old
woman.

That caught her by surprise. Her strength seemed to
leave her. The mirror slipped out of her hand and dropped on the *kang* mat. After a long pause, she answered
faintly, "Coming!"

It was Auntie Zhao. She was one of those people on
whom fortune seems to smile. Blessed with a large
family of children and grandchildren, all honest and
hard-working, she managed her house in a strict yet
open-minded way. She had let the wife of the eldest
son run the house for ten years now, stepping in only
when there was a quarrel among the younger wives. So
they all respected her, and she had time and energy
enough to throw herself into the co-op's activities. As
she always treated others in a friendly, unassuming way,
in spite of being older than most of them, the villagers
had a high regard for her. She looked upon the youngsters as her own children or grandchildren, but never
spared her breath when she felt criticism or praise was
due.

As soon as Dajie opened the gate, auntie scolded, "What's the meaning of this? The sun's up high now, but your gate's still shut, the whole yard's in a mess. Is this the way a wife should behave? You young people. . . ."

Setting foot in the courtyard, she rapped out again, "Just look! All this dirt and mess, isn't it a disgrace?"

Once in the house, she frowned and fulminated, "Well I never! For shame! So slovenly! This time of day, yet your quilts are still not folded, the place isn't tidied, the child's still crawling about in his birthday suit. . . . Do you call this a room? I call it a fowl run! You've turned this cosy nest into a shambles. And what for? Oh, I get so sick of you young wives. . . ."

Dajie asked auntie to sit on the *kang* and began to fold up the bedding, saying sullenly, "Auntie, I'm fed up with this life! I'd rather close my eyes, jump into the river and be done with it."

"Oh, nonsense! Don't talk such rubbish. Aren't you afraid you'll offend the gods?"

"I must be paying for some sins in a past life: why else should I have such a wretched time of it now? Auntie, you don't know, first thing in the morning of the Spring Festival. . . ."

Auntie Zhao cut her short. "It's all your fault," she said. "If you hadn't hurt his feelings so badly that day, it wouldn't have come to this. Seeing you going for each other like this really wrings my heart. All right, I'll go and fetch him back presently."

"No, don't. It's my own fault. I did the wrong thing. I shouldn't have agreed to take him in the first place, but it's too late now to cry over spilt milk."

The child began to bawl. Picking him up she gave

him her breast, then drying her tears continued, "Look how he's let me down! If not for me, he'd have starved or frozen to death. Yet now that he's been made a stockman and is well thought of, this heartless wretch has become so puffed up that he has no use at all for baby and me. Don't you call him back! I won't let him in! Haven't I had enough of his bullying?"

Auntie Zhao pursed her mouth and glanced sideways at Dajie. "*Ai,* child!" she exclaimed. "Why was it you had no quarrel all these years, yet now you come out with this talk of being bullied. Your auntie knows what's troubling you. Don't be silly. You know the old saying, 'Men must make their way in the world.' You can't keep him tied to your apron-strings. You won't find another good honest chap like Chengxu, not even if you look for one with a lantern. Besides, see how well he's done these last few years. He can go in and out of the county court and sit talking on equal terms with County Head Liu and Secretary Yang."

"I couldn't care less if he sat on a golden throne. He can go ahead and enjoy his wealth and honour, I'm quite content with my pickled cabbage soup. I've gone through enough in the past three days to last me for the rest of my life."

"It's not that your auntie likes to scold, but you're not being fair. You complain about feeling blue these last few days, but he's having a much worse time! Eating a snack or drinking a bowl of soup with different families. . . ."

"He's born to be a beggar. Even if he had a golden bowl, he'd go begging with it. What can I do?"

"I should really slap you, you know! Don't you ever talk such nonsense again. You've no idea where he's been sleeping these nights. Instead of a *kang* he has a door-board propped on two troughs with not so much as a roof over his head. His quilts are wet with snow. An ox broke loose the other night and did its business right by his ear, only just missed his mouth! Last night a donkey and a mule went for each other. They'd just been fed together and weren't used to each other. In their scuffle they kicked over the board he was sleeping on, smashed it. . . ."

Wide-eyed, Dajie asked anxiously: "Oh-h! Was he hurt?"

"You should know. . . ."

"Where is he hurt? Is it serious, auntie?" She had a sinking feeling. "Why didn't you tell me before?"

Auntie smiled and said calmly, "You should know, anyone else would have been hurt, beyond a shadow of doubt. But not Chengxu. He thinks so much about the cattle that he sleeps with one eye open, so to speak, and jumps up at the slightest stir. If it had been someone else, the mule would surely have kicked the donkey to death!"

Dajie heaved a sigh of relief, then changed her tone again, "If I'd been the mule I'd have given him some good kicks on the backside."

"You said it yourself. I can see that you're a fire-brand. When you're together, ten to one you're the one that stirs up the trouble."

Dajie's face flushed red. She realized her slip and tried to cover it up. "You know, I didn't really mean that. In fact, I don't care whether he's alive or dead. He's only himself to blame. A snug room and a warm *kang* mean nothing to him. What can I do? He's completely wrapped up in those animals. He loves to sleep with a cow at his feet and a calf in his arms. What can I do about it? I can't grow two more legs."

"I can hardly believe my ears, the nonsense you talk. Aren't you afraid of being laughed at?" So saying auntie got down from the *kang*. "You wait here while I fetch him back for you."

"Auntie, you keep out of this. I'm not going to let him just step in so easily, I can tell you. If I don't stand firm this time, how's he going to treat me later?"

Auntie made a show of anger. "I'm going to call the tune this time," she snapped. "You'll listen to me, whether you like it or not. I don't hold with the idea that what your elders say doesn't matter any longer. I'm going to fetch him this minute. If he's offended you, let him apologize. If you don't want him to work on that job, let him give it up. There's no such thing as a couple never clashing, but how can you keep storming at him like this?"

After seeing auntie out, Dajie hurried back. She dressed the child in his new suit made for the festival, took up a toy rattle from the *kang*, and pushed it into his hands for him to play with. Then she went out, drew a pail of water from the well, fetched some wood, boiled the water, washed and scoured all the cooking utensils and bowls, and gave the furniture, doors and windows a good scrub. The house had had a spring cleaning before the festival. The paper on the top part of the window was new, with bright red paper-cuts pasted on it, while below were two panes of glass, each about one foot square. Four New Year pictures were pasted on the wall over the *kang*. After this final cleaning, the gloomy house immediately brightened up, looking just as it should at the Spring Festival. She then took up a broom and went out to the courtyard. The sun was shining brightly. It was now getting on for noon. There was not enough time to give the place a thorough sweep, so she simply swept the middle of the yard and the gateway. All this was done in a few moments, for she was incredibly quick and deft in her actions.

"What shall I cook for dinner?" Dajie wondered. "The old man selling beancurd won't have gone yet. Why, some dumplings! We didn't have dumplings even on the day of the Spring Festival." She put down the broom to wash her hands, then taking some small change from under her pillow and a large bowl from the table she went out.

Dajie was well-known in the village for her smartness and dexterity. Her lot in life, however, had previously aroused sympathy. At the age of seventeen, she had been brought to Nanzhao in a bridal sedan-chair. The next year, she gave birth to a boy. The following year her husband chopped off his own fingers to avoid being conscripted by the Kuomintang, but then he contracted tetanus and died. Dajie nearly cried her heart out. And worse still before her tears were dry, that same winter, pneumonia carried off her child. How unjust life had been to her! These sudden disasters striking in close succession weighed heavily on this helpless girl, not yet twenty, who had practically no experience of life, nor any preparation for suffering. How could she bear it? How could she live on? Would it drive her out of her mind? Her neighbours were worried about her and shed tears for her. But she did not go mad, indeed she could not afford to, because she had to look after her mother-in-law. This poor woman of over sixty, having lost her only son and grandson too, had no one else to depend on. Dajie still had her parents and she was young; but who would support this disconsolate old widow? So Dajie hid her tears to comfort her mother-in-law, working as hard as she could to keep the wolf from the door. She learned how to farm, to sell her produce at the fair, to deal with debt collectors and court runners. Once she was hauled to court for failing to pay the land rent and drafted to dig trenches. Some of this young widow's neighbours had nothing but praise for her. The less sympathetic often made cutting comments.

Her patience and timidity changed into shrewdness and aggressiveness. As she was still so young and had no children, her mother-in-law, with tears in her eyes, had urged her to remarry, but she had refused. One day at dusk, she came back from her work in the fields to find the food ready, but her mother-in-law was nowhere to be found. She called several times without getting any reply. She became apprehensive. Then she noticed that the door of her mother-in-law's room was tightly shut and heard a sound from inside. She peeped in through a crack in the window and screamed with horror. Forcing open the door, she flung her arms round the old woman, realizing that she was attempting to hang herself to free Dajie of the burden of looking after her. They mingled their tears then, lamenting their cruel fate.

Soon afterwards, things took a turn for the better due to the arrival of Zhao Chengxu, Dajie's present husband. The old people said he had been a homeless waif, leading a vagabond life, till he begged his way to Nanzhao fifteen years before. At first he worked as a servant for a landlord, then went off to work with an old stockman called Chang. As he had no name, they gave him the name Zhao Guantao.

In the last month of the year of Dajie's misfortunes, Zhao Guantao was sent packing and went back to Nanzhao Village to find what odd jobs he could. Some go-betweens urged Dajie to marry him, and she had no strong objection as she knew him to be hard-working and had long had a good impression of him. Nevertheless, she hesitated, being afraid people might gossip about her for remarrying before the customary three-year period of mourning was over. Just then, some of her relatives who were rich peasants butted in to veto this marriage to a man who was not native-born. Dajie was stung to the quick. "You didn't do a thing when I was in difficulties," she thought. "You didn't stretch out a helping hand when we had nothing to eat, but treated me as if I were a total stranger. Now you expect me to defer to you as my elders! I suppose you're waiting until ma dies to sell me, and rob us of these few *mu* of land." So she made up her mind, with her mother-in-law's approval, and despite all opposition married Zhao Guantao. And from that time on, he changed his name to Zhao Chengxu, Chengxu meaning to carry on the family line.

Her mother-in-law died six months after they were married. And things became steadily more difficult until the liberation of the whole mainland. Then life improved for them, especially after the rent-reducing movement and the land reform. The young couple worked hard to found their family fortune. Chengxu was young and strong, and a good hand at farming. Dajie was no weakling either. No matter what the task in hand, she worked alongside her husband and saw it through to the end. Besides this, she spent the evenings spinning and weaving cloth to sell in the market. In this way, she kept herself busy from one year's end to another, never idling for a single day. And as things became better for them, smiles and youth came back to Dajie.

Now the custom in a household like theirs at this time was for the wife to control all financial matters; so Dajie was naturally the head of the house. It so happened that Chengxu was a man of few words. He only knew how to get on with the job in hand and was quite willing to leave all decisions to her. "Do whatever you think fit," he used to say. So for the last few years Dajie had had her own way and done just as she pleased to her great satisfaction. It was only recently that things had begun to change.

During the last two or three years, Chengxu had learned to read and write in the literacy class and he was roped into all the village affairs. After some time he not only spoke at meetings but also took to reading the newspaper as well. Then, just as Auntie Zhao had said, he could sit talking on equal terms with the county head. Dajie was very glad, proud of having such a good husband. When a boy had been born to them the winter before last she felt life could hardly be better. She just wished her husband would spend more time at home, to dandle the baby, light the fire, and chat over the events of the day with her. Chengxu, however, did not seem to care for such things. He spent most of his spare time outside, studying or attending meetings. Although Dajie felt disappointed, she never nagged him.

The previous winter, when the co-operative was set

up, she had joined it without hesitation. As she and her husband had such trust in each other, they had never talked it over seriously, and that was how the present trouble had started. They had both joined the co-operative eagerly, but each for different reasons.

Dajie thought that since things were on the upgrade and they had a son it was time for a happy family life. It had been pretty tough for them before the setting up of the co-op. Back from a day's hard work, they had had to cut grass, clean the sty, and feed the cattle; but now with the co-op, the cattle would be taken care of collectively. In the daytime, they could work in the co-op's fields. In the evenings, they could sit comfortably together, she doing some needlework or learning a few new characters, and they could chat, or take the child into town to see a show. How happy and contented they would be! She lost no time in carrying out her plans. The day after the cattle were sent to the pool, she asked Chengxu to remove the manger from the cattle-shed, lay a thick layer of fresh earth on the ground and tamp it thoroughly. Then the walls were replastered with fine mud. A few pieces of furniture were installed. So everything should have been fine!

However, things worked out quite differently. Chengxu had been elected vice-chairman of the co-operative and also head of the cattle section. That was nothing to get keyed up about. The trouble was that he also agreed to be a stockman. It was like this: the co-op members were all concerned about the cattle. The first people chosen for the job had not proved satisfactory, but when Chengxu offered to take it on everyone was happy. Some families who had rubber-tyred carts and sturdy, barrel-chested horses and mules now joined the co-op too, because they knew that Chengxu, who had worked for wealthy landlords and handled plenty of cattle, was hard-working and reliable. He was the right man to look after their animals. But Dajie was most put out. Besides, at this stage, some members of the co-op were not yet used to the regulations governing the use of the cattle. They didn't handle the cattle carefully, and Chengxu had offended them by taking them to task. A few had said a lot of harsh things about him, not even sparing Dajie. Chengxu turned a deaf ear to it all, and stuck to his guns. Dajie, however, couldn't bear this sort of abuse. She put all the blame on her husband.

"You're barking up the wrong tree. There are lots of other things to do in the co-op, why don't you do something else?" she asked.

"Then who's to take care of the cattle?"

"You simpleton! You think the co-op will go to pieces without you? No one thanks you for it. Can't you hear them snarling at you all over the place?"

Chengxu grunted, "Let them. . . . But I won't allow anyone, no matter who he is, to mishandle the cattle!"

"Doesn't it make your cheeks burn, all that foul talk?"

"No," Chengxu answered calmly.

"Well, I can tell you, it does mine," she muttered, clenching her teeth.

"Just pay no attention," he replied just as calmly.

"But what's the point of it all? What will you get out of it? So many people are at logger-heads, can you guarantee the co-op won't go to the dogs, the cattle won't lose weight?"

"We must see to it that the co-op is well run, and

that not a single head of cattle is lost. That's what most people say," argued Chengxu. "Since they think I'm the man for the job, I can't back out. The people here have always been very good to me. Now that this co-op has been set up, they think I can do some useful work and they've asked me to take care of the cattle. And since this is the only job I know, shouldn't I do my best at it to help build up a socialist Nanzhao?"

After this argument, Dajie felt something was wrong. The more she chewed the thing over, the more convinced she became that Chengxu had changed. He had once been a man of few words, but now he was always preaching to other people. He had once done whatever she asked, but now he no longer said, "Do whatever you think fit." The small world within the four walls of the house didn't seem large enough for both of them now. They seemed to be standing one inside the wall, the other outside. Was she demanding the impossible? No! She just wanted an ordinary family life. Couldn't she have such a simple thing? Yes, she should have it. She should. She was the head of the family, after all!

On the afternoon before the Spring Festival, Chengxu came home late, because he had waited to dose the grey mule with medicine. Everything was ready at home to celebrate the festival, but Dajie sat on a corner of the *kang*, spinning, glum-faced and withdrawn, colder than a stone statue. Chengxu immediately sensed that something was wrong.

"Is dinner ready?" he asked with a smile.

There was no answer.

"I was held up a little; I'm a bit late, I know. Let's eat now, shall we?" he said with another smile.

"The pigs have all been fed!" she snapped at him.

"Who are you angry with?" he asked, still smiling.

"With myself!" She yanked the thread so hard that the yarn broke.

Not venturing to say any more, Chengxu lifted the cover of the cooking pot. The pot had been washed and some cold water poured in it. He then went to the cupboard and searched in it for a while, without finding anything. Evidently she had left him nothing to eat. He shot a look at Dajie, who ignored him as if they were strangers and went on spinning. Then in a jar he discovered some tempting looking snow-white steamed rolls. But as these were for the festival, he dared not touch them. At last, he found some cold hard corn-flour buns in a small pottery basin, and ate these with some peppers from the cupboard. He tossed out some cheerful remarks while munching, trying to draw her into conversation.

"Uncle De's cow's about to calve," he said.

Whirr, whirr, whirr . . . went the spinning-wheel.

"Haven't you taken a course in the new midwifery?" he joked.

Whirr, whirr, whirr . . . went the spinning-wheel.

Not daring to say any more, he ate the cold food in silence, fetched some bucketfuls of water, then returned to the stockman's hut.

That night, Dajie heated the *kang* till it was hot, changed the bedding and quilts, took the new clothes out and put them under the quilts so that they would be warm to wear the next day. Then, having rocked the child to sleep, she settled down besides the lamp to start making dumplings for the festival. While doing this, she was thinking of the warning she had given her husband that afternoon, and of his recent attempt to humour her. She was sure she had brought him to his senses now, and he would come home early, say some pleasant things to her, and then. . . . The more she thought of all this, the happier she felt. "I made him smart this afternoon, but as soon as he comes back tonight he can stuff himself with dumplings." But when the dumplings were ready there was no trace of him. The water was boiling, still he hadn't turned up. She sat there on the *kang*, biting her finger-nails until the kerosene in the lamp ran out and the boiled water became quite cold, but there was no sound at the door and no one came in. Dajie was on tenterhooks. She decided to go to the cow-shed. It was near, on the other side of their courtyard wall; but to reach it she had to go round to the next lane, as there was no gate through their north wall. She lit a small lantern and went out. The sky was dark, stars were twinkling high above, and because it was so late all around was still.

When she reached the next lane, she saw three people with lanterns coming out of the stockman's hut. One of them was Zhao Fengwa, a stockwoman. She flashed her lantern at Dajie, saying mischievously, "I'm so sorry, but Chengxu and I have agreed that I'm to go home."

Dajie did not answer her but went to the cow-shed. She quietly lifted up the straw-matting that hung over the door, and squeezed in. All the windows were tightly shut, a pile of wood was burning briskly. The smoke-laden air was almost suffocating. Chengxu, hugging something in his lap, was sitting with his back to the door beside a cauldron.

"What on earth are you staying here for?" Dajie flared up.

On hearing her voice he turned round. "So it's you!

Coming here at this hour!" he said in surprise. Then in great excitement he burst out: "Come quickly and look!"

"What is there so good to look at?"

"Our co-op has had a windfall. We're sure to have a bumper harvest next year," Chengxu said. "Look, a calf born to the old cow on the night before the Spring Festival. And a bull calf, too. Isn't it a lucky omen?"

It was only then that Dajie saw the calf in his lap. He was stroking its soft wet hair.

"See what a nice colour his coat is! As red as fire!" Chengxu exclaimed in admiration.

Dajie glanced around the shed and saw that the cow, her head down over a wooden tub, was lapping up some thin gruel. The quilt over her back she immediately recognized as one she had made herself. Chengxu explained, "She's like a human. While she's 'lying in' I mustn't let her catch cold. So I let her use it. It doesn't matter. As I'm here, I'll see to it that it doesn't get dirty."

Dajie was happy and embarrassed at the same time. Torn between anger and amusement, she retorted, "Don't you have a family? Do you know what it is today? It's the eve of the Spring Festival."

"But how can I leave here? Fengwa wanted to go back, and someone has to be here to see to things. You go back first. Don't bolt the door."

Dajie was smouldering. She turned and went out reluctantly, forgetting to take the lantern. It was pitch dark outside, as she stumbled along the rough road. Suddenly, a burst of noise followed by a flash in the dark sky made her start. Then there was the noise of firecrackers being let off by those who were celebrating the festival early.

Chengxu didn't go home until the next morning. Dajie's glum and drawn face warned him that a storm was brewing. In silence he laid the table, then went to make the fire. Dajie put the dumplings into the cooking pot and ordered sternly, "Light it!"

Chengxu hastily started working the bellows.

"Not so fast. It's bubbling over."

At once he stopped.

"Keep going! Why have you stopped? Can't you go slowly?"

Chengxu manipulated the bellows carefully, and remained silent. A few moments later the dumplings were dancing in the cooking pot. He damped the fire down, then moved to the table. Dajie was holding a bowl of dumplings in her hands. Just as he reached out to take it, she plonked the bowl down, splashing hot soup on his hands and shaking the dishes on the table. Chengxu felt his blood rise, but tried hard to control himself. "*Ai*! Can't you be more careful?"

"What? Doesn't it suit you here?" Dajie glared at him. "Then go somewhere you like better. Nobody is stopping you. It's you who came begging to be taken in here. I didn't send you an invitation card!"

When she first started scolding and grousing Chengxu was able to control himself. But then, she really let herself go, like a string snapping, pouring out the whole story of Chengxu's vagabond life. He didn't even know his own father's name, she jeered, but was fated to be a beggar. While working off steam, she never stopped to think how wounding her husband must find this. That was brought home to her when she heard a crash. She saw soup flowing past his feet, dumplings bouncing all over the floor, and chips of the bowl flying in every direction.

"What's the idea on the Spring Festival. . . ." But as she turned round her reproaches stuck in her throat, so startled was she by the sight of Chengxu's white face, his trembling hands and quivering lips. He was unable to speak. His cheekbones stood out above his hollow cheeks and his eyes were flashing. Dajie was frightened, not knowing what he would do next. He bit his lips, raised one arm, but didn't touch her. Instead, he slowly pushed back his chair and stepped out of the room. She watched him walk away, feeling at a loss.

He had not been back since, and that was three days ago.

In these three days, Dajie had been thinking. She had felt pangs of conscience and cried for shame. She often mumbled to herself, "He can say what he likes to me, even hit me. Anything would be better than this." She couldn't help going out and inquiring about where he was having his meals, or where he was staying for the night. She would often cook something and take it to a neighbour, asking her to give it to Chengxu to eat, without letting him know where it came from. The neighbours told Auntie Zhao of all this, which was why she had gone there to sort out the trouble.

Dajie was sitting on the *kang* again making dumplings. These dumplings meant even more to her than the last. While her fingers were working nimbly, she thought over the events of the past few days. She reviewed all that had happened before to her as well as others, weighing its meaning. She realized that she was in the wrong. Now and then she looked through the window at the north wall, and listened intently for any sound on the other side of it. She bent her head low, racking her brains as to what her next move should be.

After a while, she heard rustling in the courtyard. She lifted her head and saw a tall, broad-shouldered man with a prominent forehead and a firm jaw, his eyes keen and penetrating. With a big wooden rake in his hand, he was stacking up the hay scattered by the chickens. He was working in silence, without even glancing in her direction. The joy she felt was not unmixed with annoyance. She wrenched her eyes away from him and gazed at the ceiling instead, pouting. The rustling continued. It was such a temptation to look again that soon her eyes turned back in Chengxu's direction. He was giving the yard a thorough sweeping with a large bamboo broom. Another couple of strokes and it would be clean. The courtyard seemed suddenly spacious, the sunshine streaming down on it brilliant and warm. Chengxu laid down the broom, and went over to replace some stones that had fallen off the wall of the pigsty, still in silence, not once glancing in her direction.

Dajie's pout became more pronounced, she fixed her eyes most resolutely on the ceiling. A sudden slapping sound made her look outside again. She saw that Chengxu had taken off his black waistband, and was using it to beat the dust off his clothes. He was now advancing with measured gait towards her door. For a moment she panicked, then regained her composure. She turned her back to the door, staring at one corner of the room. Footsteps approached her, then stopped. She pretended not to have heard them. Head bent over the board, she busily kneaded the dough. The silence was suddenly broken by the clatter of the carrying-pole and the pails. She stole a glance around, but he had gone.

All she glimpsed was a pail disappearing through the doorway.

The large jar was replenished with fresh water pail after pail, while Dajie sat staring at the corner at the sleeping child. She was wondering what was the right thing to do. Finally when she was through with the last dumpling, she heaved a deep sigh, as if she had come to some important decision.

Auntie Zhao came in at this moment. On seeing how the two of them looked she called out, smiling, "Eh, you're both grownups now, why do you sulk like children? Dajie, is your back so pleasant to look at? Turn round!"

"Auntie! Come and sit on the *kang*." Dajie turned to greet her eagerly with a smile. But actually, her eyes had flashed past auntie's shoulder to meet those of Chengxu. Her glance was reproachful, as if to say, "Don't you know you've got a home to come back to?"

"Aha! Dumplings! For me?" asked auntie merrily.

"Of course!" said Daije. "Who else would they be for!"

"Now, now, no fibbing. I know the truth of the matter." Auntie turned towards Chengxu and continued, "Thanks to you, I'm in luck. You'd better take my advice next time, instead of ignoring it."

"I've never ignored your advice," he answered, laughing.

"That's the way. Well, I must be going," auntie said.

"No, how can you just walk out like this?" they protested. Dajie pushed her back to the *kang*, and Chengxu went out to fetch faggots.

When he had left, auntie whispered into Dajie's ear, "Don't worry. I've given him a good talking-to. He didn't argue back, but kept saying he was wrong to have smashed that bowl on the Spring Festival of all days. And I've just been to the co-op head. He says they only considered the fact that he's a man the co-op can't do without, but they forgot about you. The co-op committee will think up some better arrangement."

She broke off there because Chengxu came in with the faggots and sat down at the cooking-range to make the fire. When the water boiled, Dajie stood beside the cooking pot, putting the dumplings in. She didn't complain about the fire this time. It seemed as if, after three days, Chengxu had become an expert in handling the fire.

A piece of dark oil-cloth was spread on the *kang*, on which the dishes were placed. Auntie sat on the *kang*, leaning back against the wall, saying, "Chengxu, you come up too." He took off his shoes then and sat beside her.

Dajie brought over a bowl of dumplings and put it in front of auntie. Next she took up the bowl which her husband always used. Then Chengxu began to speak, affably and slowly but gravely and firmly too, as if he had prepared a speech for some formal occasion.

"Don't get me anything to eat yet," he said calmly. "We have to get things straight first, so that you don't snatch the bowl away again!"

There was tension in the air as he continued, "Any work for the co-op that I can do, I will do. They want me to take care of the cattle and I'm not going to stand out against them. Nothing can change my mind about this!"

An oppressive silence ensued. Auntie opened her eyes wide, her face all screwed up, glancing from one to the other. Then she suddenly put down her bowl and chopsticks and cried, "What on earth are you saying? Are you trying to blacken my name? To make me look a fool, eh? What did I tell you? You didn't listen."

Dajie, however, kept her presence of mind. "Auntie, don't get excited," she said calmly. "Let him go on, let him finish."

Auntie scolded Chengxu, "Husband and wife should talk things over together. No one's like you, so stubborn and uncompromising."

Chengxu took this without any sign of being perturbed. Just then the child woke up and called, "Papa!" Chengxu picked him up and hugged him, caressing his head gently as he looked at Dajie, waiting for her answer.

She asked, "Are you through? Go on. Get everything off your chest, since auntie is here."

"That's all I want to say."

"All?" she snapped back. She scooped up some dumplings before continuing, "The solemn way you started, I thought it was going to be something really important."

"I just wanted to make this clear, for fear you might get wrong ideas," he said.

Dajie put the large bowl of dumplings in front of him, dried her hands on her apron and said heatedly, "Don't underestimate me! I've weathered some storms in my life; I'm not a weakling. You want socialism. So do I. And I love the co-op just as much as you do. If you sail the sea, I'll be rowing in the same boat. If you climb mountains, I'll be at your heels. I'll follow no matter where you go, you can be sure of that!"

Auntie had been on tenterhooks at first, not knowing whether this was another squabble or they were coming to terms. She sat there in a quandary with no idea what to do. Chengxu was gazing curiously at Dajie, trying to fathom her meaning.

"What are you staring at?" she asked. "Never seen me before? Or didn't you get me? Do I have to say it a second time?"

"No!" he said hastily then took up the bowl and said, "Auntie, the food is getting cold, let me give you a fresh helping."

She picked up the bowl and said, smiling: "No, no. The food's not cold. It's only that I can't make out whether the two of you are blowing hot or cold!"

Three days later, a small gate appeared in Dajie's north wall. This gate linked up her tiny enclosure with the outside world. North of the gate was the stockman's hut of the Red Banner Co-op. Further north again were two rows of sheds, one on the left for oxen and cows, the other, on the right, for horses and mules. Between the sheds was a big gate, through which, across a lane and an open yard beyond, could be seen a vast expanse of wheat fields extending to the river bank. The last traces of snow had disappeared, the fields were green with young wheat. Men and women co-op members in threes and fives were starting the spring raking. Fresh warm breezes played leisurely over the fields and lanes. The courtyard before the stockman's hut was bathed in all the splendour of golden sunlight. Chengxu had taken off his padded coat and was busy getting in dry earth. Dajie was standing beside a trough, and mixing feed for the cattle with the stick she had thrown over the wall three days ago. Their small son was playing on the stacks of hay, sunning himself.

Chengxu finished his task of wheeling in the dry earth, took the child up, and went over to his wife. Looking at the feed, he said critically, "Don't pour the bran in too quickly. Stir it thoroughly. Remember the old saying, 'With bran or no, to four corners the rod should go'."

Dajie pursed her lips and cast a knowing glance at Chengxu, as if to say, "Huh! You think you're the only one who can do things properly!"

The child paid no attention to his parents, as he was busy playing. But when Chengxu leaned forward to tickle the nose of a calf with a straw so that it leaped away, shaking its ears, the little boy laughed with glee and urged his father to run after the calf.

October 1956

Translated by Wen Xue

The son of a schoolteacher, Wang Wenshi was born in Ronghe County, Shanxi Province in 1921 and began writing lyrics and yangge *operas in the 1940s. Since the fifties, he has published the full-length opera* Comrades-in-Arms, *the short story*

The Night of Wind and Snow, *the novella* Black Wind *and the popular stories* New Acquaintance *and* The Dunes.

Wang is now vice-chairman of the Xi'an branch of the Chinese Writers' Association.

The Family on the Other
Side of the Mountain

Zhou Libo

TREADING on the shadows of the trees cast on the slope by the moon, we were on our way to a wedding on the other side of the mountain.

Why should we go to a wedding? If anyone should ask, this is our answer: Sometimes people like to go to weddings to watch the happiness of others and to increase their own joy.

A group of girls were walking in front of us. Once girls gather in groups, they laugh all the time. These now laughed without ceasing. One of them even had to halt by the roadside to rub her aching sides. She scolded the one who provoked such laughter while she kept on laughing. Why were they laughing? I had no idea. Generally, I do not understand much about girls. But I have consulted an expert who has a profound understanding of girls. What he said was, "They laugh because they want to laugh." I thought that was very clever. But someone else told me that "although you can't tell exactly what makes them laugh, generally speaking, youth, health, the carefree life in the co-op, the fertile green fields where they labour, being paid on the same basis as the men, the misty moonlight, the light fragrance of flowers, a vague or real feeling of love . . . all these are sources of their joy".

I thought there was a lot of sense in what he said too.

When we had climbed over the mountain we could see the home of the bridegroom — two little rooms in a big brick house. A little ancient red lantern was hung at the door. The girls rushed inside like a swarm of bees. According to local tradition, they have this privilege when families celebrate this happy event. In the past, unmarried girls used to eavesdrop the first night of a friend's marriage under the window or outside the bridal chamber. When they heard such questions as "Uh . . . are you sleepy?" they would run away and laugh heartily. They would laugh again and again the next day too. But there were times when they could hear nothing. Experienced eavesdroppers would keep entirely silent on their own first night of bliss and make the girls outside the window walk away in disappointment.

The group of girls ahead of us had crowded into the door. Had they come to eavesdrop too?

I had picked several camellias to present to the bride and groom. When I reached the door I saw it was flanked with a pair of couplets written on red paper. By the light of a red lantern one could make out the squarely written words:

> Songs wing through the streets,
> Joy fills the room.

As we entered, a young man who was all smiles walked up to welcome us. He was the bridegroom, Zou

Maiqiu, the storekeeper of the co-op. He was short and sturdy with nice features. Some said he was a simple, honest man but others insisted he wasn't so simple, because he found himself a beautiful bride. It is said that beautiful girls do not love simple men. Who knows? Let's take a look at the bride first.

After presenting the camellias to the bridegroom, we walked towards the bridal chamber. The wooden lattice of the window was pasted with fresh paper and decorated in the centre with the character "happiness", cut out of red paper. In the four corners were charming papercuts of carp, orchids and two beautiful vases with two fat pigs at the side.

We walked into the room. The girls were there already, giggling softly and whispering. When we were seated they left the room in a flock. Laughter rang outside the door.

Then we scrutinized the room. Many people were seated there. The bride and her matron, who was her sister-in-law, sat on the edge of the bed. The sister-in-law had brought her three-year-old boy along and was teaching him to sing:

In his red baby shoes a child of three,
Toddles off to school just like his big brother.
Don't spank me, master, right back I shall be
After going home for a swig of milk from mother.

I stole a glance at the bride, Bo Cuilian. She was not strikingly beautiful, but she wasn't bad looking either. Her features and figure were quite all right. So we reached the conclusion that the bridegroom was a simple and yet not too simple man. Though everyone in the room had his eyes on the bride, she remained composed and was not a bit shy. She took her nephew over from her sister-in-law, tickled him to make him laugh and then took him out to play for a while in the courtyard. As she walked past, she trailed behind a light fragrance.

A kerosene lamp was lit. Its yellowish flame lit up the things in the room. The bed was an old one, the mosquito-net was not new either and its embroidered red brocade fringes were only half new. The only thing new were the two pillows.

On the red lacquer desk by the window were two pewter candlestands and two small rectangular mirrors. Then there were china bowls and a teapot decorated with "happiness" cut out of red paper. Most outstanding of all the bric-a-brac presents were two half-naked porcelain monks, with enormous pot bellies, laughing heartily. Why did they laugh? Since they were monks they should have considered such merry-making as frivolous and empty. Why had they come to the wedding then? And they looked so happy too. They must have learned to take a more enlightened view of life, I suppose.

Among the people chatting and laughing were the township head, the chairman of the co-op, the veterinarian and his wife. The township head was a serious man. He never laughed at the jokes others cracked. Even when he joked himself, he kept a straight face. He was a busy man. He hadn't intended to come to the wedding. But since Zou was on the co-op's administrative staff and also his neighbour, he had to show up. As soon as he stepped into the door, the bridegroom's mother came up to him and said:

"You have come just at the right moment. We need

a responsible person to see to things." She meant that she wanted him to officiate.

So he had to stay. He smoked and chatted, waiting for the ceremony to begin.

The head of the co-op was a busy person too. He usually had to attend at least two meetings a day and give not less than three serious talks. He also had to work in the fields. He was often scolded by his wife for coming home too late at night. He was hard working and never complained. Indeed he was a busy man, but he had to come to congratulate the union of these two young people however busy he was. Zou Maiqiu was one of his best assistants. He had come to express his goodwill and to offer his help.

Of all the guests, the veterinarian talked the most. Talking on all subjects, he finally came to the marriage system.

"There are some merits to arranged marriage too. You don't have to take all the trouble of looking for a wife yourself," said he, for he had obtained his beautiful wife through an old-fashioned arbitrarily arranged marriage, and he was extremely satisfied. With his drink-mottled pock-marked face, he would never have been able to get such a beautiful wife by himself.

"I advocate free choice in marriage," said the chairman. His wife, who married him also in the old-fashioned way, often scolded him, and this made him detest the arbitrary marriage system.

"I agree with you." The township head sided with the co-op chairman. "There is a folk-song about the sorrows caused by the old marriage system."

"Recite it to us," urged the co-op chairman.

> The old marriage system promises no freedom.
> The woman cries and the man grieves.
> She cries till the Yangzi River overflows,
> And he grieves till the green mountain is crested
> with white.

"Is it as bad as that?" laughed the co-op chairman.

"We neither cry nor grieve," said the veterinarian proudly, looking at his wife.

"You are just a blind dog who happened on a good meal by accident," said the township head. "Talking about crying reminds me of the custom in Jinshi." He paused to light his pipe.

"What kind of custom?" asked the chairman.

"The family who is marrying off a daughter must hire many people to cry. Rich families sometimes hire several dozen."

"What if the people they hire don't know how to cry?" asked the veterinarian.

"The purpose is to hire those who do. There are people in Jinshi who are professional criers and specialists in this trade. Their crying is as rhythmic as singing, very pleasing to the ear."

Peals of laughter burst forth outside the window. The girls, who had been away for some time, evidently were practising eavesdropping already. All the people in the bridal chamber, including the bride, laughed with them. The only persons who did not laugh were the township head and the veterinarian's beautiful wife who knitted her brows.

"Anything wrong with you?" the veterinarian asked softly.

"I feel a little dizzy and there's a sick feeling in my stomach."

"Perhaps you're pregnant?" suggested the township head.

"Have you seen a doctor?" the bride's sister-in-law asked.

"She's in bed with a doctor every night! She doesn't have to look for one," laughed the chairman.

"How can you say such things at your age!" said the veterinarian's beautiful wife. "And you a chairman of the co-op!"

"Everything is ready," someone called. "Come to the hall please." All crowded into the hall. With her little boy in her arms the bride's sister-in-law followed behind the bride. The girls also came in. They leaned against the wall, shoulder to shoulder and holding hands. They looked at the bride, whispered into each other's ears and giggled again.

On one side of the hall were barrows, baskets and bamboo mats which belonged to the co-op. On the table in the centre, two red candles were lit, shining on two vases of camellias.

The ceremony began. The township head took his place. He read the marriage lines, talked a little and withdrew to sit beside the co-op chairman. The girl who acted as the conductor of ceremonies announced that the next speaker was to be one of the guests. Whoever arranged the programme had put the most interesting item, the bride's turn to speak, at the very end. So everyone waited eagerly for the guests to finish their chatter.

The first one called upon was the co-op chairman. But he said:

"Let the bride speak. I have been married for more than twenty years and have quite forgotten what it is like to be a newlywed. What can I say?"

All laughed and clapped. However the person who walked up to speak was not the bride but the veterinarian with his drink-mottled pock-marked face. He spoke slowly, like an actor. Starting from the situation in our country before and after Liberation and using a lot of special terms, he went on to the international situation.

"I have an appointment. I must leave early," said the township head softly to the co-op chairman. "You stay to officiate."

"I should be leaving too."

"No, you can't. We shouldn't both leave," said the township head. He nodded to the bridegroom's mother apologetically and left. The co-op chairman had to stay. Bored by the talk, he said to the person sitting beside him:

"What on earth is the relation between the wedding and the situation at home and abroad?"

"This is his usual routine. He has only touched on two points, so far. There are still a lot yet."

"We should invent some kind of device that makes empty talkers itch all over so that they have to scratch and cannot go on speaking," said the chairman.

After half an hour or so, the guests clapped hands again. The veterinarian had ended his speech at last. This time the bride took the floor. Her plaits tied up with red wool, she was blushing crimson in spite of her poise. She said:

"Comrades and fellow villagers, I am very happy this evening, very, very happy."

The girls giggled. But the bride who was saying that she was very, very happy didn't even smile. On the contrary, she was very nervous. She continued:

"We were married a year ago."

The guests were shocked, and then they laughed. After a while it came home to them that she had said married instead of engaged because she was too nervous.

"We are being married today. I'm very happy." She paused and glanced at the guests before continuing. "Please don't misunderstand me when I say I'm happy. That doesn't mean I shall enjoy my happiness by sitting idly at home. I do not intend to be a mere dependent on my husband. I shall do my share of work. I'll do my work well in the co-op and compete with him."

"Hurrah! And beat Zou down too." A young man applauded.

"That's all I have to say." The bride, blushing scarlet, escaped from the floor.

"Is that all?" Someone wanted to hear more.

"She has spoken too little." Another was not satisfied.

"The bride's relative's turn now," said the girl conductor of ceremony.

Holding her boy of three the bride's sister-in-law stood up.

"I have not studied and I don't know how to talk." She sat down blushing scarlet too.

"Let the bridegroom say whether he accepts the bride's challenge," someone suggested.

"Where is the bridegroom?"

"He's not here," someone discovered.

"He's run away!" another decided.

"Run away? Why?"

"Where has he run to?"

"This is terrible. What kind of a bridegroom is he!"

"He must be frightened by the bride's challenge to compete."

"Look for him immediately. It's unbelievable! The bride's relative is still here," said the co-op chairman.

With torches and flashlights people hurried out. They looked for him in the mountains, by the brooks and pools and everywhere. The co-op chairman and several men, about to join in the hunt, noticed a light in the sweet potato cellar.

"So you are here. You are the limit, you. . . ." A young man felt like cursing him.

"Why have you run away? Are you afraid of the challenge?" asked the chairman.

Zou Maiqiu climbed out of the cellar with a lantern. Brushing the dust from his clothes he raised his eyebrows and said calmly in a low voice:

"Rather than sit there listening to the veterinarian's empty talk, I thought I might as well come to see whether our sweet potatoes are in good condition."

"You are a good storekeeper, but certainly a poor bridegroom. Aren't you afraid your bride'll be offended?" said the chairman half reproachfully and half encouragingly.

After escorting the bridegroom back, we took our leave. Again treading on the tree shadows cast by the moonlight, which by now was slanting in the west, we went home. The group of girls who had come with us remained behind.

In the early winter night the breeze, fragrant with the scent of camellias, brought to our ears the peals of happy open laughter of the girls. They must have begun their eavesdropping. Had they heard something interesting already?

November 1957

Translated by Yu Fanqin

Zhou Libo was born in 1908 in Yiyang County, Hunan Province and studied in Shanghai where he joined the League of Left-wing Writers. While working as an editor on Literature Weekly, *he began to write essays and reviews and to translate Russian literature. After taking part in the land reform movement in the northeast in 1946, he produced his important novel* Hurricane, *which won a Stalin Literary Prize. He subsequently published numerous novels and collections of short stories.*

Before his death in 1979, he was chairman of the Hunan Federation of Literary and Art Circles, chairman of the Hunan branch of the Chinese Writers' Association and a member of the national committee of the Fifth Chinese People's Political Consultative Conference.

Father and Daughter

Luo Binji

IN the days before the course of the Shu River was changed, the people of Yu Village and thereabouts had a hard time of it. Even when no drought came to dry up the crops in the mountainous regions, Yu Village never reaped much of a harvest, for floods plagued the land every year. If people were lucky with their wheat harvest, they were likely to lose their soya-beans later in the summer. Fortunately they had a market every three days, and this was the main shopping centre for the area east of Maling Mountain. So most of the villagers depended on the market for a living. Here they could trade in sea-food, salt, pig-fodder and so on. Many of them owned bean noodle mills. Their noodles were well known and found a market in Xinhailian to the east and Xuzhou to the south. Some of the villagers kept a shop, some dealt in livestock and others were traders, taking whatever prawns or croakers the pedlars of other villages had to offer, selling them in the market and paying afterwards. In a word, everybody had his own means of livelihood and crop-raising was a secondary matter.

On market days, the peasants poured along the big roads and small paths which led to Yu Village from all directions. Some started from their homes with their pigs at the first cockcrow. The fish pedlars had passed the night on the way; at daybreak they still had a mile or two to go before they would reach the market. There were people with baskets on poles, others with wheelbarrows, and cloth pedlars on bicycles piled high with cloth at the back. They were certainly skilled cyclists, the way they hailed their acquaintances as they went. "I didn't see you yesterday at the market in Xia Village," one would say to another. "I sold my two barrow-loads of fish in no time." There were also pedlars with rubber-tyred barrows. As soon as they reached the market they opened up their boxes and hung coloured ribbons from the framework built on the barrow. But whether they were pink or green, the ribbons were all faded like the paint in old temples. There were also faded towels, embroidered pillow-cases, scarlet quilt-covers and so forth. At the front was hung an advertisement for Two Sisters' Brand hair oil. It was really a fetching arrangement. And in the glass cases on the cart were powder, rouge, hair-nets and pins, buttons, silk thread, mirrors with a yellow crescent moon on the glass, painted combs and what not. . . .

Now let us turn to Xiangjie who had a regular stall at the market which sold bowlfuls of hot beancurd beneath the old locust tree. She came originally from Guan Village, but she had been married to a man of Yu Village when she was seventeen. In the second year of marriage she bore her husband a son — now a small boy of seven. Her husband died within three years. Her means of support were three *mu* of land she received in the land reform and the beancurd-making outfit her husband had left her which included a grindstone, a donkey, thirty-six black porcelain bowls and three tables with benches under the old locust tree. All she had to buy was beans. The legs of the benches and tables were set in the earth, just logs with boards nailed across them.

Next to Xiangjie's stall at the market there would always be an old man selling a few vegetables. As soon as his business was done he would gather up his scales and baskets and come over to Xiangjie's booth. Never absent from his hands were his pipe and his black cotton tobacco pouch adorned with a jade pendant. He came to help, he said, but his tongue was busier than his hands. When he saw a bowl emptied, he called, "The customer is paying, Little Stone." If anybody asked for more seasoning he called again, "Pass the jar, Little Stone." Occasionally he might pass the bowls himself, that is to say, holding his pipe in one hand he took the bowl of beancurd from Xiangjie with the other and gave it to Little Stone without leaving his seat. "Mind," he would say, "don't drop it." This was Xiangjie's father, Old Man Xing from Guan Village. Sitting there in his long gown, he looked more like a tutor from the village school than a vegetable-grower. What pleased him most was to hear people praise his grandson. If somebody from another village remarked, "What a clever boy! How old is he?" He would reply, "Seven. He's my grandson," fingering his beard and looking very contented. But if anyone remarked that Little Stone's eyes were as beautiful as his mother's, the old man used to turn away and begin a conversation with someone else as though he had not heard. "Has your soldier written home?" he would say. "Is he still serving in the fifth regiment?" In short, he did not like his young widowed daughter to be praised.

Xiangjie was a noticeable person in Yu Village. Though her delicate eyebrows, straight nose and full lips were not in themselves anything out of the ordinary, they set off her dark eyes in such a way as to give the whole face a very pleasing look. But in the depths of the bright eyes, there was a cool shadow of indifference. Looking directly into them, you found them very distant. Clearly this was not her natural character but something she had developed after long years of widowhood. Usually she dressed in black trousers and a high-collared, tight-sleeved tunic, also black. This way of dressing among the young women of southern Shandong had been the fashion in Beijing at the time the old republic was set up about forty years ago. The collar was so high that it hid half of her ears. She wore her hair in a smooth chignon with a lock at one temple brushed softly behind her ear. Her trouser legs, sleeves, and collar were all slightly fringed. She tied her hair and trouser legs with black ribbons and on market days a black apron was added. All this black heightened the effect of her fair skin, and gave her an ethereal look.

She did a brisk trade. Everyone in the market who had any spare money liked to drink a bowl of hot bean-curd at her open-air stall in the same way city folk like to drink coffee or milk in cafes on Sundays. Old men would often make a special trip to the market with their small grandsons for the beancurd, which was so hot that beads of sweat stood on their noses when they were drinking it. The seasoning was red peppers fried in sesame oil, golden and appetizing, and warming to the tongue. As customers left the stalls they used to

smack their lips and say, "Good peppers, very hot!"
Xiangjie felt very happy, as she watched the departing
figures. A small smile would appear on her face as
though to say, "Why must you add so much pepper-oil?"
Some elderly long-standing customers who liked nothing
but a little more salt in their beancurd praised neither
the peppers nor Little Stone but Xiangjie instead. "Ten
more years, and you'll have seen it through. Your son'll
be able to support you then," and "She really *is* capable,"
they would say. To these words of encouragement in
the feudal tradition which seemed to drug her and bury
her youth, she showed no reaction, not even as much as
when her peppers were praised, though one could see
in her eyes a repressed feeling of pride and contentment.
Of course there were also impudent young strangers
among her customers who loitered around with empty
bags after they had sold their grain, having caught sight
of Xiangjie in her black suit as they passed by the big
locust tree. They used to whisper to each other and
then squeeze into a vacant seat. Staring at Xiangjie's
beautiful eyes, they loudly called for beancurd but did
not even notice when Little Stone handed them the
bowls. Then they would ask about her in lowered tones,
yet loud enough for her to hear. When they found the
local customers eyeing them angrily they fell into a guilty
silence, and finally left in resentment. At times like
these Xiangjie would adopt a serious air and keep her
eyes averted. It was clear that she held these people
in contempt. In short, she was apparently the ideal
woman of feudalism, and was often held up as a model
to those women who thought to marry a man of their
own choice. These women, mostly active members of
the women's association, emerged after Liberation with

the collapse of the landlord class. They had made a deep impression upon Xiangjie, who in those days often went to their discussion meetings behind her father's back and listened to reports on the part women were playing in production, the struggle for equality between men and women and free choice in marriage. Although she sat silent in the meetings, staring hard, her black eyes sparkled and she laughed so readily that Xiangjie the young girl was brought to life again. It was during these days that Old Man Xing discovered a tiny yellow flower in her chignon. It did not please him and he wanted to say something but he hesitated to speak. As he was leaving that night he could restrain himself no longer. "Take that bit o' grass out of your hair. Throw it away!" he said, turning back at the door. "Look at yourself! Who is it meant for? I really don't like to have to raise such a question." Xiangjie seemed suddenly to wither. She stood with downcast eyes, silently fingering the blossom which she had taken from her hair.... The old man left, then returned before he reached the gate.

"What good can it possibly do you to pick up ideas from those women of the young women's corps? They have no sense of reserve in front of men at all. Isn't it shameful?" he added in a kinder tone as if feeling sorry for having scolded her and to show that he was only concerned for her good.

The yellow flower turned quicker and quicker. A tear rolled down her cheek and dropped on to her finger.... Old Man Xing left feeling satisfied.

After that incident Xiangjie's face resumed its mask of indifference and looked as if she had lost her zest for life. She knew that if she acted according to her own wishes with the support of the women's association, she would be sure to lose the approval of her father and the respect of those around her. If her father should break with her, how was she going to live? A woman was like a vine, she thought, and a vine couldn't live without the support of a tree. If she was to lose the respect people had for her she couldn't stand the slightest breeze. There was Little Stone to be thought of, too. "It would all straighten out when he was grown up. But what a long time it would be!" she often sighed and mused in the small hours of the night.

2

Old Man Xing, though thin as a ginseng root and very frail in appearance was strong for his sixty-seven years. He seldom fell ill or needed medicine. His mouth was hidden behind grey whiskers. His eyes were sharp and yet unhappy. He would gaze moodily into the distance and his face would become as expressionless as stone. He did not work as a peasant all the year round. In his youth, he sold rope and persimmons in autumn, cherries in spring, and fruits and other sacrifices for the Weaving Maid in the seventh lunar month. All the money he earned he spent on his mouth. He liked to smoke fine tobacco from southern Shandong, drink green tea and sugar his water-melons. He was very cowardly, too, and was known to have done only one adventurous thing in his life. That was when he joined a group of black-market pedlars in a salt-smuggling expedition. It was a pitchdark night of the kind that smugglers liked — so dark that you couldn't make out who it was, even though they stood in front of you.

When they passed through the customs barrier they had to lie down on the ground and listen to the footsteps of the patrols as they passed. Unfortunately they lost their way. As they were trying to get their bearings they suddenly heard a shot. All the smugglers squatted down as if trained to it except Old Man Xing who promptly took to his heels. But it was only a shot fired into the air by some peasant who had taken them to be people stealing their maize. After that he was the laughing-stock of the village, and even to this day was regarded with contempt by the younger generation. Besides, he was clumsy with the plough and could not even spread manure properly. The household and farm chores were all done by his wife, Mama Xing.

Mama Xing was over sixty. According to herself, she was already buried up to the neck. But she was strong for her age. Although her hair was grey, she had the ruddy complexion of one who works in the open air all the year round. Her jacket was patched at the shoulders and the sleeves were always rolled up to the elbow as if she had just finished salting vegetables and was now going to cut grass. She was respected by everybody in the village. When they received two *mu* of land and a well in the land reform Mama Xing took to growing vegetables. She grew cabbages, spring onions, cucumbers, egg-plants and whatever was in season. For the climbers she built supports of hemp stalks and for the delicate plants she put up windbreaks on the north. And squatting beside her, handing her hemp or barley stalks was Old Man Xing. He was only her assistant. When the plants needed water, Mama Xing would push the waterwheel around while Old Man Xing made little channels with a shovel for the water to flow through the garden. Sometimes he wasted a lot of water by not making the channels properly. "Why don't you put your tobacco pouch away for a bit," Mama Xing would say at such times. "Nobody's going to pinch it from you." Sometimes she would add, "What you're going to do when I'm gone, I don't know!"

"What ever makes you talk like that? How can you go before me?" Old Man Xing retorted.

"Who knows? If it should happen that way how are you going to get on? I'm really worried for you."

"It can't happen that way," he said with a reproachful look. "Enough of such nonsense! You frighten me when you talk like that."

Mama Xing laughed happily. She looked on him as an old baby, and liked to tease him. There were only themselves and their one daughter. They had no relatives at all in Guan Village.

Guan Village was only two *li* from Yu Village and people in one village could hear the cocks crowing and the dogs barking in the other. So Old Man Xing often visited Xiangjie. He used to come, pipe in hand, on the evenings before market day when Xiangjie was making beancurd. When there were weddings in Guan Village, and Mama Xing was given wedding cakes, he wrapped them in a 'kerchief and thrusting them into the front of his gown to keep them warm took them to his little grandson. They lived so near to each other that on moonlit summer nights Old Man Xing would come over after dinner to drink tea at his daughter's and chat with the uncle of Xiangjie's late husband and go back when it was time for bed.

Xiangjie's uncle was a fish trader who went under the

nickname of Rat. With his narrow face and close-set eyes he really looked like one. He respected Old Man Xing, and in return, Old Man Xing respected him. The friendship between them was treasured by Old Man Xing, for it was of a type he could not get in Guan Village. Xiangjie's third guest was eighty-one-year-old Liu Zexing, formerly a livestock dealer and smuggler of salt and opium. He was a big fellow with a head as round as a wine-pot. It was said that all the money he had earned was long since squandered on women in other villages, for he had come back empty-handed. He now sold wine and cooked pork at the market. He often brought along a handful of tea so that Xiangjie could make tea for them. On the days when she made beancurd the three friends would drink a big bowl of hot bean milk. On those days the room was always steamy. A big bag was hung above the stove from which bean milk dripped down into a pot. Old Man Xing squatted in front of the stove helping to add fuel. As a matter of fact, only his lips were working, asking, "Is the milk all right?" and "Is it time to put the salt in?" or ordering Little Stone to bring him some more maize stalks. He looked busy enough but all the time he was actually waiting for his daughter to say that the bean milk was ready. Then Little Stone would fill the bowls and the three old men would sit around a big ladle by the side of the stone-mill. Then excitement sparkled in Old Man Xing's cold eyes. This was his happiest and most comfortable time, as if it were his well-earned rest after some very hard work.

As they began to drink and smoke, they would chat about the latest events in the village market. Someone had bought some eggs for his daughter-in-law after the birth of her baby, one said, but the first one he opened was rotten, in the second the yolk couldn't be distinguished from the white, and what do you think the third was like? There was a chicken inside! "Who did he buy them from? Couldn't he get his money back on the next market day?" asked Old Man Xing.

"But you don't know which village he came from," remarked Xiangjie's uncle, "and I don't suppose he'll have the nerve to come again."

The eighty-one-year-old livestock dealer held a different view. "You can't blame the seller. The buyer should know better. Why must he buy from this pedlar when there are so many others?"

"He must have been after the cheapest price," observed Xiangjie on the side.

"That's right! So how can he blame others?" the livestock dealer reaffirmed. Everybody thought this a wise comment, so they shifted their topic to episodes of people losing large profits by being covetous of petty advantages. Xiangjie's uncle told them that it was easier to trade in Yu Village than in Xia Village, because the people in Xia Village were cunning and always took advantage of strangers. Take the man who came there to sell dried shrimps. As soon as he put down his baskets, he was surrounded by a crowd of women and children. One wanted half a catty, another eight ounces. Then they began their game. The shrimps were handed out, and money was handed back. Then the person who handed him the money began demanding his shrimps. It was then discovered that he had given the shrimps to a woman and received the money from a man!

"Yes, it's very hard to deal with the people of Xia

Village," said Old Man Xing. "Every time I sold cherries there I knew I'd be bound to lose a few catties no matter how hard I watched. They are dishonest. I think they should be educated, now we've got liberation."

But the livestock dealer again held a different view. "Oh, about the shrimp seller that was his own fault. How can you blame others if you don't charge before giving out the shrimps? You have to be sharp. If money can be earned so easily everyone would go peddling." Once more he was considered right.

Xiangjie took a delight in all this chit-chat but nothing interested her more than their comments on the big annual fair at Jiqi Mountain. Whenever the conversation turned to the fair she would remember the actor who played the role of the young lover in *Picking up the Bracelet*. How he had flirted with Sun Yujiao with his eyes! Such clever eyes! And how he had twiddled the handle of his fan with his two fingers! The happy times of her girlhood which were gone for ever came back to her and she sighed happily.

The three cronies also gossiped about the village officials and exchanged news of the villagers who were in the army. Now they took a great deal of interest in the recent quarrel between the leader of the peasants' association and his wife.

"Why, no wonder! He was out at meetings till midnight, wasn't he? And she had to get up to answer the door every night. Well, anyone would get fed up with that," commented Xiangjie. But Liu Zexing the eighty-one-year-old former livestock dealer said, "He led the movement of raising the status of women. That's a queer business! Now he can't control his own wife any more. She'd never have dared to quarrel with him before the Liberation."

"She certainly wouldn't," agreed Old Man Xing. "Her husband would have slapped her across the face before she could answer back." Xiangjie had to admit that all this was true and that there was nothing more to be said.

The three old men, hardly noticing they had drunk the bean milk, smoked and sighed comfortably and contentedly. Any evening when one of them failed to appear, the others would be in low spirits as if something dear to life was missing. They would begin to fuss, and send Little Stone to look for him. If he happened to be the livestock dealer, Xiangjie would be concerned for his health. She pitied him for having to fetch his own water and carry his own earth for repairing his house. He had seen luxury before. He was just not one to complain, that's all. If it were her husband's uncle she would worry whether he had quarrelled with his daughter-in-law. She felt sorry for the old man and also for the daughter-in-law who was living alone. Her husband had been conscripted by the Kuomintang, and had been away for six years! During the Huaihai battle they hoped that he would be captured and sent home by the People's Liberation Army. But they had not heard a word of him. Anyway, when there were only two old men, they swallowed the bean milk even more noisily, especially when it was Old Man Xing's turn for the ladle.

Generally speaking, they were contented. Happiness and the relaxation of peaceful times showed on their faces. War was very far from this area. With the elimination of the landlords, the heavy taxes which had crushed the peasants were done away with for good. Besides, they had received land and this gave them a source of livelihood. So what cause could they have for discontent? What could they complain about? All this showed itself in their cheerful faces and their idle gossips. Of course, we are talking here of how things stood in 1949 before the Shu River changed its course.

3

That spring, at the time of the busy season in the fields, Xiangjie set out one day for the Xia Village fair ten *li* away. As she put the soya-beans to soak for grinding that morning, she remembered that it would soon be the time for the farmers getting beans in for seed. They had been in short supply at the market lately, and prices would be bound to rise, so she must buy them early. This was in the days before the government had brought in the policy of planned purchase and distribution. Every district had its joint supply and marketing co-op, but this was not enough to keep the food market stable. As a sharp business woman, Xiangjie naturally had foresight. When she went, she left Little Stone in charge of the house and told him if he wanted to go out and collect herbs for the pigs, he should lock the door and leave the key under the piece of rock by the pig pen.

Xiangjie rarely went far from home except to visit her parents during the New Year and on other festivals. When she wanted to buy beans from Xia Village she usually asked friends to get them for her, that is, if they were not too busy in their fields. This time, she decided to go herself, because she found that those who usually went to the market had already gone, and she feared that prices might rise if she left it any longer.

As she had left in a hurry, she wore the same black cotton jacket and trousers she usually wore at home, with a padded suit underneath. Her trousers were neatly tied at the ankles with two black ribbons. The only difference was that she wore a pair of black cotton shoes embroidered with red peonies. She carried a sack twisted around her hand and her finger still wore the thimble that she had forgotten to slip off. Was it because she hadn't been anywhere for so long, or was it the south wind bringing the feel of spring and the songs of the lark? Xiangjie had felt flustered when she started out, but as she went along she was struck by the freshness of the air and the beauty of the open spaces outside the village.... Suddenly she was reminded of her girlhood when, basket on arm, she had gone to collect wild vegetables. She was filled with a sense of exhilaration, as though it was a holiday.

As she walked along she saw a man at the cross-roads ahead turn in on the road for the Xia market. From the back, he was tall and broad-shouldered, and he wore a leather strap around his peasant tunic. A black cap sat on his head and he strode along in the manner of a man sure of his dignity. Indeed, it was by his walk that Xiangjie recognized him immediately as Zhang Da, the captain of her village's militia. His tunic and cap merely confirmed her conjecture. There was no other in an area of eight to ten *li* around who had such a bold stride.

Zhang Da was at one time an agricultural labourer who could crack a whip with a flourish and sing splendidly in the Laiwu dialect. In the past, when he met a young woman, he would redden up and became tongue-tied. Since he had joined the Communist Party during the land reform, he wore a habitually serious expression. Because the class struggle was still acute and complex, with the well-to-do peasants still wavering, he had learnt the value of caution. After the militia under his command had taken part in a battle against the Kuomintang troops and been cited for their good fighting, he adopted a martial air. He developed a long stride and a loud voice. Even though he might be talking to only one or two people, he would shout at them as if he were addressing the whole of the militia. Those who didn't know him used to think he was playing the bureaucrat, but others knew that his eardrums had been damaged by blast during battle, and that though he was not completely deaf, he could not catch anything said in a low voice and accordingly thought of others as being like himself. He commanded a high prestige among the militia. His courage and resourcefulness were known far and wide.

This twenty-six-year-old bachelor attracted the general attention of the marriageable young women of Yu and other villages nearby. Some made no secret of their admiration, even in his presence, and openly tried to court his favour. But he gave them no encouragement. In time, those who had once idolized him came to actively dislike him. "Huh! What's all the fuss about?" some of them said publicly. "I can't see that he's anything out of the ordinary!" And if someone said, "Ssh! ... He might hear you," they would retort, "And what if he does? I want him to!"

Undoubtedly Xiangjie, too, was infected with the general atmosphere of hero-worship. So, when she met him now, face to face, she was secretly overjoyed at this unexpected good luck, and hailed him aloud: "What are you hurrying for? Have you got someone waiting for you at the market?"

Zhang Da stopped and turned. "I've only just finished watering my plot, so I'm a bit late," he said. Then he added, "You look happy today. Are you going there too?"

"Why! Can't I go unless I look happy?"

"But I've never seen you at the Xia market before."

"You wouldn't have seen me even if I'd been there, there are so many people."

"Wouldn't I? I'd always see you, even from far away, if you were there," he said, looking amiable.

"So your eyes are quite different from other people's?" joked Xiangjie.

"I don't think so," said Zhang Da, walking with her shoulder to shoulder but looking straight ahead in a more guarded manner.

"Then how could you spot me from so far?" Xiangjie gazed at him as though to search his heart.

"Why not? I'm sure I could," he parried.

"Have I a distinguishing mark on my face, then?"

Zhang Da's defence collapsed and he guffawed. "How could you?" he said. Can this be the woman who used to be so conservative and backward? He thought to himself. He would never have dreamed she could be so provoking and so quick with her tongue. His thoughts went back to the time when, as a young girl, she had once been his ideal — of course she had known nothing about it; what a pity it was she made no progress politically. After Liberation, the distance between them had lengthened more and more. It seemed he had forgotten the existence of such a girl who had once attracted him so greatly.

"Does Little Stone's granddad come to see you often?" he asked, changing the subject.

"He does," said she, lowering her head, apparently still absorbed with their earlier trend of talk. When she raised her head again, she was more tranquil. "If it wasn't for his granddad living near and able to come over often and give a helping hand, I could hardly manage."

"So you think you're able to live like this because of his support?"

"Who else could I depend on, if not on him?"

"Did you have any land before the Communists came? And who does he owe for the easy life he now lives?"

"That's true of course. . . ."

Perhaps Zhang Da did not hear, or perhaps he did not want her to continue, for he kept on: "Could you run a stall in Yu Village market if the Eighth Route Army were not stationed nearby? You said you depended on him. Did he ever fetch any water for you, or push the grindstone when you were making beancurd? I would say it was he who's done well out of you."

"To say nothing of other things," he continued. "What about the pigs' dung? How much does he make away with in a year!" He said this in such an indignant tone, and with such an air of conviction, that Xiangjie dared not say anything to the contrary.

"Oh yes," she said naively. He is quite observant, she thought. Even the old man making away with a few barrow-loads of pigs' dung had not escaped him.

Zhang Da's interest in her welfare evoked a sense

of gratitude in her. She accepted his words not as a reproof, but as the sincere advice of a friend.

"You mustn't let yourself be influenced by the backward elements all the time. There, am I right or not?"

"How do I know if you haven't said it to me?" she murmured blissfully.

Actually, Zhang Da did not quite catch what she said, but he could see that she was happy, and could sense that he had won her full trust. Such trust and submissiveness put him in the position of a protector. He had never felt this way before any other young woman, so strong and upstanding. If I can teach her some politics, he thought, she might join my mutual-aid team and quickly become an activist among the women. He fixed his eyes at her appreciatively.

"Why do you look at me so?" she said. "Don't you recognize me?"

"You seem to me quite different today," said Zhang Da frankly. "You don't look in the least like you did in Yu Village market. What has made you so happy?"

"Nonsense," said Xiangjie smiling. "How can I look different? I am still myself."

"But it's true!" said Zhang Da seriously. "You don't look at all like you did when I saw you in Yu Village market."

"How do I look, then?"

"You look like —" said Zhang Da ponderingly. "You look like you did when I saw you at the Jiqi Mountain fair that year."

"When was that?" pursued Xiangjie, as if something precious hung on their conversation. She looked all attention, her eyes shining as though she was trying to remember. Thereupon, Zhang Da said it was the second year after the Shu River breached its dike, adding that it was the year he began work as an odd-job man in another village and there was talk of her being married to a man of Yu Village. She had been wearing a red blouse that day, and a pair of silver earrings. She had been standing behind the enclosure of a shop, quite a distance from the stage. All this he said in a loud voice as if he was addressing the militia. "Could you see what was going on on the stage from that distance?" he asked.

Now there is a saying, "He who always talks is thoughtless, but he who always listens has an object in view." It was applicable to these two. While Zhang Da took it to be a casual chat, Xiangjie understood it as something quite different. She completely ignored his question as to whether she could see the stage clearly, and turned the conversation to where he was that day.

"Why didn't I see you?" she asked curiously.

"Who was worthy of your attention in those days?" Zhang Da burst out laughing. "Nobody! So why should you have seen me?"

"You make me sound like some sort of a goddess!"

"Well, if you'll have it that way," said Zhang Da, looking at her and laughing.

"But I think you're the only one who thinks that way."

"What did you say?"

"I said — well, nothing!" At this juncture, Xiangjie seemed to rise from a state of drunkenness. "Good heavens!" she exclaimed, stopping short and looking around. "Where are we? Isn't this Wang Family Graveyard we're coming to?"

Zhang Da also halted, turning his head in all directions with arms akimbo, like a commander inspecting the position. "How could we've come here in broad daylight?" he cried aloud.

They had missed their turning. Xia Village was to the northeast, but they had headed due east.

"Let's go back," said Zhang Da with a wave of his hand, pausing to give a final glance around as if to verify the fact that they really had got to the south side of Xia Village.

"What sort of leader are you?" Xiangjie broke into a ringing laugh.

"How did it happen!" Zhang Da smiled. "We must have been woolly-brained to have come to these graveyard woods."

Suddenly, for the first time, the two of them felt completely happy and contented. Laughing and out-of-breath, Xiangjie kept teasing him. "What sort of leader are you? Someone must have bewitched you," she complained, as if she herself had kept her wits about her. In fact, Zhang Da had been following her. But he took it all in good part and laughed with her. Xiangjie laughed until the tears came to her eyes. "You looked so baffled standing there with your arms akimbo!" she gasped. "What were you looking for? Ghosts?"

At each new gibe, Zhang Da rocked with laughter. They were like a couple of drunkards, Zhang Da rolling along with an unsteady gait. As soon as they got on to the main road and sighted Xia Village, they saw people coming towards them from the direction of the market, wine bottles in hand. They quietened down, especially Xiangjie, who composed herself and adjusted her chignon for fear of betraying any sign of impropriety.

Zhang Da sensed she had recovered the detached look which she wore in the Yu Village market. But when her eyes met Zhang Da's a surreptitious joy was still discernible in their depths.

"Now you go ahead!" she said. "And wait for me by the well at the village entrance when you return."

How had they reversed roles? When did she acquire the confidence to issue orders to the militia captain? Without knowing why he accepted them, Zhang Da strode off obediently. And having completed his assignment for the mutual-aid group, he brought with him the yoke, the halters and harnesses and waited for her by the well at the village entrance.

They were not on their own on their way back from the market. There were altogether five people, including Xiangjie's uncle, well known as a trader in the Yu Village market. He had disposed of some remaining bloaters in the Xia Village market and was now walking along in a leisurely fashion with the two empty baskets slung on to a pole on his shoulder. There was also an old woman who peddled hairnets and embroidered shoe uppers in the Yu Village market, grumbling all the way for having brought an insufficient quantity of red silk thread, saying that she could easily have sold another three or four ounces! The five fell naturally into two groups as soon as they were out of Xia Village, Xiangjie and the old woman dropping to the rear. The old woman was carrying a small white cloth bundle, while Xiangjie walked empty-handed. The bagful of beans she had bought had been taken home earlier by a neighbour who had come from Yu Village with a wheelbarrow. Although Xiangjie was walking slowly, her face was as flushed as if she had been sitting in front of a fire. This aroused the curiosity of the old woman pedlar, who kept looking at her every now and then.

"Do you feel all right? You had a drop to drink in the market, didn't you?" she asked.

"No," Xiangjie instinctively put her hand up to her cheek. "I put on too many clothes this morning. It's hot!"

She walked on with her head down. It was clear she had something on her mind. The people in front were drawing farther away. She had started out at a brisk pace and had only slowed down when the old woman said, "We're going too fast, it's no use trying to keep up with the men." It was late in the afternoon when she reached home.

Xiangjie was very restless that evening. Her ears pricked at the slightest sound — a footfall outside the compound, the noises of the passers-by, a cock crowing and the pigs squealing. At one moment she would run into the courtyard as though to take a look at the pigsty, standing there as if listening for something. The next moment she would grab a pole and run to fetch water, though the jar was more than half full. She felt as though Zhang Da was always about her, that she would run into him at any time and any place. She was tense, and felt that she must see Zhang Da, to confide to him an important secret which, however, did not exist. She only knew that she wanted to meet him again. Not until darkness fell did she come to her senses. She was surprised at herself. How could I be so unsettled? she thought to herself. Was I haunted by a ghost from the Wang Family Graveyard? Had one of them followed me home? With this reflection she began to cool down.

But she did not take off her embroidered shoes and continued to sit on the *kang* listlessly.

There was a ring from the doorbell. It was her father paying her his usual visit. His arrival reminded Xiangjie that it was time to harness the donkey for the grinding. For the first time she felt irked by the thought of Old Man Xing. Why should he come when it was so late? she thought. He always came as soon as it was dark, never giving people a moment of peace.

"What? No one at home?" she heard her father call from the courtyard. Usually it was her custom to hail him from behind the paper-framed windows with "Is that you, dad?" as soon as she heard the ring at the door and the sound of his tread. This was something the old man liked, for it made him feel that she was there waiting for him. But this time it was different. He had shut the door in the courtyard and stood there for quite a while listening for the sound of his daughter's voice or the stir of the donkey hauling the grindstone. He thought she was not at home. Then he heard her say, "I'm in the house, come in," in a cold tone, quite unlike her usual one. Perhaps she was tired, he thought, for he had been told by her uncle whom he met as he came into the village that she had been to the market. Or perhaps she was cheated over the beans? When he entered the room, Xiangjie was changing her shoes. After asking a chain of questions: "How many beans did you buy? Was there a good supply? What was the price? Has Little Stone gone to his evening class? Did he collect some pig-fodder today? he ensconced himself as usual on the wooden block outside the track of the grindstone.

As Xiangjie was harnessing the donkey, the old livestock dealer Liu Zexing came in, stool in hand.

"Now, try this," he offered Old Man Xing his tobacco pouch.

"Mine's not so bad!"

"Ah, you don't buy the kind of leaves I'm smoking!"

In fact, Liu Zexing knew very well that they both bought their tobacco from the same place, but he still thought his was better. And Old Man Xing also knew the tobaccos were the same, yet he too thought that Liu's tasted milder. It was altogether inexplicable.

Before long, Xiangjie's uncle, Liu Si, turned up with his grandson. He knew the Yu Village market day fell on the morrow, so he could look forward to a bowlful or two of bean milk that evening. He was very proud of his twelve-year-old grandson, saying that his legs were now as round as rafters and inviting Old Man Xing to feel them. "Just feel his bottom, he's a real fatty! And look at his legs, you know all about it when he kicks you!" Then he asked, "Have you finished up your planting yet?"

"Not yet," replied Old Man Xing. "I've only got a couple of rows of leeks in so far, and I'm paying for them with my legs, already!" Then he added, "Unless you count the couple of rows of tomatoes. . . ."

"What do you want tomatoes for? You like to eat 'em?" asked Liu Si, the pedlar. "Who'll you sell 'em to? To my mind, you'd do better to plant more cabbage, they'll fetch more money."

"Now you talk like that because you're outside of the trade," said Liu Zexing.

Old Man Xing rapped his pipe on the floor and said, "Do y'know what price they fetched when they were

first put on the market last year?" he asked. "I'd planted two rows. When I brought them to market, I cut
the price down to five *fen* per catty. The district work-
team in West Swamp scrambled to buy 'em. I saw I'd
been a fool. So I raised the price to seven. And I sold
the last three or four lots for eight a catty. Nothing
much to speak of in the way of taste, just a sour bagful
o' seeds. Not the sort of things a land worker cares
for!"

"How much do you expect to make off your land if
you depend on the work-team as your sole customers?"
asked Liu Si.

"There're the people from the district health station,
aren't there? And the county inspection team, too;
they'll be down during the wheat harvest, won't they?
Well, they'll all buy. It's only us who won't!"

"Won't huh?" said the eighty-one-year-old ex-horse-
dealer. "It's because we don't know how to prepare
'em, that's why! If you don't know how to go about
'em, not even a sea-slug'll taste good."

"Now the right way to eat tomatoes is with sugar,"
he continued. "You can't do without sugar. Half a
catty of sugar to one catty of tomatoes, and the sour
taste's drowned. Well, they eat like water-melon then,
sweet and crisp, nothing could be nicer!"

"All right," said Liu Si. "When the tomatoes are
ready, let's get half a catty of sugar and try 'em out.
We'll have a go, too. Hey, what d'you say?" The last
sentence was addressed to his grandson whom he dan-
dled high in the air.

"You've got to have the top-grade sugar of the Xia
Village co-op, too," remarked Liu Zexing. "That stuff
that hawker Xiao Wu touts around at the market won't

do. What sort of sugar is that any way, half of it mixed with fried flour. A catty of the co-op's sugar goes twice as far."

"Things are not too good nowadays for the small traders," said Liu Si, expanding on the topic. "You know, the co-op came along with half a cartful of dried shrimps in the Xia Village market today and the price dropped by two *fen* a catty."

"I'm afraid when the next fish market comes around," he continued, "the co-op'll have a go at that, too. It'll be like the way they brought their cloth to the market, a couple of baskets on each bicycle. It doesn't give others much of a chance!"

"How many people are there in the co-op?" said Liu Zexing. "Why don't they go to the smaller markets farther away? Still, they can't bring a thousand and one things to the market. If they trade in bloaters, then you can go in for carp. If they sell plates, you can sell pots. There's plenty o' leeway still. Would a man let his way be barred by a bit of a wall?"

All such conversations had constituted an indispensable part of the mental life of Xiangjie, and she used to derive great pleasure from them. It seemed to her that her life was enriched when she listened to these arguments and discussions. But today they sounded quite remote and boring. Moreover, she now drew quite different conclusions from their talk, such as, "If it were not for the co-op, how could we buy cloth, dried shrimps and salted fish so cheaply!" Of course, she kept these thoughts to herself. Then she remembered how Zhang Da had spoken of Old Man Xing on the road. "Yes," she thought. "These old 'uns are real stick-in-the-muds, fussing all the time about prices falling for this or that article, and the co-op coming in for a share, as though times are getting worse instead of better. And look at the trousers he used to wear in the winter — rotten old threadbare things." She meant Liu Si. In a word, thoughts that never would have entered her head in the past now came walking boldly in. At this juncture, she heard a stentorian voice in the courtyard: "Grinding your beans, eh?" The ladle all but dropped from her hand. Her heart leapt to her mouth, her face reddened, her mouth seemed minus the tongue. "He's come, he's come. . . ."

"Who's that?" she heard Old Man Xing ask suspiciously. The visitor walked noisily from the courtyard towards the house.

"Good evening all!" said Zhang Da loudly, entering the house. "Oh! There's quite a lot of you."

"Good evening to you," said the old men. There followed the creaking of stools being pushed back as some of them stood up to offer him a seat. Although Old Man Xing was not on very intimate terms with him, he knew he was the militia captain of the village and a respectable village cadre, and a tinge of respect was discernible in his voice as he said, "You don't come here often. So you're not engaged tonight. No meeting, eh?"

"Had a meeting already!" said Zhang Da, catching the wrong sense like those who are hard of hearing are apt to do. "We meet every day. We depend on meetings to solve our problems." He looked around with a confident air, yet without any trace of self-importance. Then he added, "Well, how are things with you, eh? I suppose you've finished up all your planting by now?" And, turning to Liu Si, "So this is your little grandson from South Swamp, eh?" And to Liu Zexing, "And how are you getting along? All right, I suppose? What were you planting in that plot of yours behind the house this morning, was it millet?"

He noticed Xiangjie smiling at him, from the shady side of the room, a familiar, affectionate smile as distinguished from the bold and tender one she had given him on the way to the market. But he did not speak to her. He settled down on the stool, looking happy and excited, quite unlike his usual stern self.

"The district committee's called upon us to wipe out the locusts," he said. "It's an urgent job. Tomorrow we'll form teams and go down to the marsh. The young 'uns in South Swamp have got their wings. If we don't get a move on, they'll take off after the rain." He wound up by saying that Bingze's mother should have come to tell this house of the call, but since she was off visiting relations, he had taken on the job of group leader for the households on the east of the village.

"I'm going to say something you won't like," said the ex-horse-dealer. "So don't get angry, because we're old friends." Then he began formally, "Now the government has started taking a hand in trade and wants to tell us what to do in the way of field work. I've never heard before of field work needing to be watched, nor did I ever hear that the land used to be mismanaged either. But people grew enough grain to live on."

"Did you ever hear the older generation say that on the day when the grain was in ear, the emperor would take his imperial plough to work his plot of one and a third *mu*? That was a sort of leadership too!" Liu Si argued.

"As I see it," said Old Man Xing, pulling at his pipe and sighing, "in the past when we didn't catch them, there seemed less locusts. Last year when we did, they came in swarms. Even spiders appeared in the wheat fields. Did the older generation ever hear of that before?"

"That's because we didn't try to catch them in the past," Xiangjie found herself arguing against her father, smiling as she did so, so as to mitigate the feeling of antagonism against him. "The insects were there, but who would have bothered about 'em?"

Old Man Xing was astonished to hear Xiangjie talk in this vein, for she had always been on his side in the past and had said that insects grew of themselves and could never be wiped out. How was it that she had changed so suddenly this evening, taking the side of the village cadre, currying the favour of an outsider against himself?

"That's true!" Zhang Da rose to his feet, looking at once grave and amiable, his thumbs stuck into his belt like a soldier. "We can't stick to our old ideas about raising crops. If we're to get bigger outputs, we've got to fight against natural calamities." Then he added, as if talking to himself, "If we want to go the socialist way, we must listen to what the Party says." One could easily see that he was accustomed to organizing the militia, who were required to observe discipline, and not used to doing propaganda among the peasants. "The task assigned by the Party has got to be fulfilled, because the Party works for the good of the people," he said emphatically.

"If the Party's concerned about the peasants, why doesn't it do something about the Shu River?" said Liu Zexing. "Every year, the beans are swept off by flood. And every family has to go without their bean sauce!

That's an important question. Why don't you cadres take it up?"

"You don't have to worry about that!" said Zhang Da in a decisive manner, in face of this back-handed challenge. Again Xiangjie backed him up.

"That's not a simple thing like building a wall or sinking a well," said she. "I should say it would be quite a job if we only have to build embankments along both sides of the river."

Now Zhang Da felt she was definitely on his side, defending him like this while the ex horse-dealer was trying to embarrass him. He fired a string of questions at Liu Zexing: "You've spent a lot of time knocking about the world, what did you bring back with you when you came home? Who gave you your land? Who gave you the relief grain for widows and widowers, 120 catties for the two seasons in the year? What did you ever get from the old society? Who built that house for you? Where did the timber come from?" he demanded angrily, fixing his eyes on the old man. Liu Zexing seemed to shrink, like a porcupine flattening its quills. He fell silent. "You're right, I came back without a rag to my name. . ." he muttered after a pause.

"All right, then!" said Zhang Da, changing to a milder tone, just as he had heard a district Party committee member do after severely criticizing him, or he himself had done after criticizing a member of the militia. The critic, perceiving the criticized had realized his mistakes, began to soothe him. "Now, you should really think this question over a bit more carefully!" he said.

Before leaving, he reminded them to bring the tools needed for catching the locusts next morning. He firmly turned down their offer to see him off and said that he would drop in to see them as often as possible. On his way home, he remembered how Xiangjie had spoken up and suddenly felt there was a strong bond of sympathy between them, more intimate than that which he experienced when they lost their way in the Wang Family Graveyard and later when he waited for her by the well of Xia Village. He cherished this feeling and began to expect certain things of her.

That night, Liu Zexing slunk off like a defeated cock much earlier than usual. But Old Man Xing stayed, seated outside the grindstone track smoking, long after his cronies were gone. Little Stone, now home from evening school, helped his mother to take the grindstone apart. Old Man Xing sat on, forgetting that he had two *li* to do to get back to Guan Village.

"Dad, time for you to go now!" said Xiangjie, after sending Little Stone to bed and placing the last stone on the trough.

"No matter, there's a moon."

"But mum'll be waiting for you!"

Old Man Xing kept pulling at his pipe. At last he called out in a flat voice: "Xiangjie!"

"What's up?"

"Lay down that broom and come over here. I want to ask you something." He sucked at his pipe again and said quietly, "What did Zhang Da come for this evening?"

"We're going to catch locusts tomorrow morning, aren't we?" said she. "Even if there was nothing on, couldn't he just come in for a chat, once in a while?"

Old Man Xing rose to his feet, gripping his tobacco pouch.

"It's all right as long as you're on the right track. Don't forget your son's so big now," he said before parting. "I can't keep you company all your life, you see. Now shut the door and go to bed!"

That night Xiangjie lay awake long after the lamp was blown out, her eyes open, thinking. Why should fate decide that she should meet Zhang Da on his way to the market, and that they should lose their way in bright daylight. Then she thought of her hilarious laughter, and of her agitation as dusk approached. It was as though she had been some other woman who had known Zhang Da for a long time. As to what Old Man Xing had said, she had not taken in a single word. Why this was so, she did not understand. One thing she knew, however, was that she had passed a day of great significance to her, and she felt blissful. Something new was beginning to take shape in her. Her father's restraint had suddenly become irksome and she knew she must break away.

4

After the locust-catching, Xiangjie met the militia captain twice more, on his own, and during the daytime. The first was an accidental meeting by the side of the well behind the village. Xiangjie attached special importance to this, for Zhang Da usually drew water from the well in the south of the village where he lived. But this time he had come to fetch water from the northern well. In doing so, he had to pass by Xiangjie's courtyard. The second meeting took place right outside her courtyard, where she had been waiting specially for the purpose.

They beamed with delight on both occasions. "This well's wonderfully clean," Zhang Da observed in his loud voice, as he drew the water from the well. "I should say so!" replied the other, smiling softly as a cat, and gazing at him with her sweet eyes. Then she made way for him and Zhang Da walked off with his two bucketfuls of water slung from a pole across his shoulder. The second time was at noon, when Zhang Da again passed her house on his water-fetching errand. "Hey! When are we going to the Xia Village market again?" he called out. "All right," she answered with a smile, her face flushing crimson.

Then for three days she missed him. At first she felt uneasy, and hung around the courtyard the whole day listening to the footsteps and voices as people passed to and fro on their way to fetch water. But Zhang Da did not come by. Xiangjie was downcast. Why didn't he come, she wondered. It was only when she learnt that he had gone to the district Party committee that she calmed down.

Undoubtedly, her uncle Liu Si knew what was going on. He had heard the remarks they had exchanged during their second meeting from the adjoining courtyard. "Are you going to the Xia Village market again?" he asked her that very evening.

"I don't think so. What can you get there, anyway?" she replied, wondering what he was getting at, and feeling all the more sickened by those old cronies and their endless talk about business.

The day after the militia captain left the village, a team of three surveyors from the Water Conservancy Bureau of Shandong Province made their appearance on the land between Yu and Guan Villages. They had with them all their paraphernalia of red-and-white scales, tripods, levelling instruments, plotting lens, and what have you. At first the peasants did not pay much attention to them. It was only on the third day, when it was announced that these people had come to prepare a new course for the Shu River, that people began to talk about it in earnest.

By this time, there was a group of people on the land between Yu Village in the south and Guan Village in the north, pouring lime water from long-necked bottles along two parallel tracks set a *li* apart and fixed by marking ropes. Quite a little crowd of people from Guan Village began to gather along the lime line in the south. Among them were Old Man Xing clad in his long robe and his wife with her sleeves rolled up to her elbows. There was another crowd from Yu Village, including Xiangjie with an apron tied around her waist, the pedlar Liu Si and old Liu Zexing, who now sold spirits and pigs' heads. A buzz of noise arose from among them, like bees on the swarm. People were gesticulating and flashing mutually infecting glances at one another. Fragments of excited, inarticulate utterances could be caught at a short distance: "But the water ghosts...!" "...Don't strike them!" "Get the cadres!" There was no telling why, but somehow somebody started heading towards a certain goal, and all ran in the same direction. Some, running with ashen faces, asked, "What's the matter?" Children, frightened, started to cry among the human stream which surged forward. The field was littered with discarded cloth shoes.

"Little Stone, Little Stone!" cried Xiangjie in a

frightened voice. She was bumped and pushed and borne along by the crowd.

The militia captain, with a rifle slung across his shoulder, suddenly appeared among the crowd. He looked tense, but calm. People began to quiet down. "Quiet, there at the back!" shouted someone. Zhang Da, one hand on hip, started in his stentorian voice: "The days of the Shu River as a trouble-maker are numbered! In the future, whatever we plant in the marshy land will be sure to give us a return. Nobody'll need to worry about having no beans to make sauce with!"

"Won't the opening of the new course mean separating Guan Village from Yu Village?" somebody asked loudly. Zhang Da recognized him — a poor peasant of Guan Village.

"How shall we people from Guan Village get to the market with the river in between?" Zhang Da saw it was Old Man Xing who had spoken.

"The Yu Village market'll be shifted to the north. Yu Village'll no longer be the centre. And when we're rid of the floods, we'll be sure to have two crops every year."

"Hurrah!"

"This time our marshy land'll be as good as the best land of Guan Village!" cried those who depended on the marshy land in Yu Village for a living, with great spirit.

All the pedlars who lived on trading in the Yu Village market, however, darted suspicious glances about them.

"How are we going to make a living if the market is shifted!" they bawled.

"And we'll have to disturb the bones of the dead!"

cried those whose ancestral graves lay within the new course.

"How about our wheat fields in the course?"

And there were such comments as: "It seems Chairman Mao doesn't care about us any more! This is inviting the devil to make trouble for us if you ask me! Directing the floods right towards our houses. . . ."

"Well said!" responded the eighty-one-year-old Liu Zexing.

Zhang Da, surrounded by the crowd, listened intently to all these utterances, breaking in time and again to answer questions, saying that "the graves will have to be moved" and "all lands will be compensated". So when he heard someone say "inviting the devil to make trouble", he swung round and swept the crowd with his eyes, noting at the same time the response of Liu Zexing.

"Who was it said that Chairman Mao doesn't care for the people around here?" he demanded sternly.

All quieted down. "Who was it, do you know?" some murmured. Others pretended to have heard nothing, and kept silent. When Zhang Da cast his eyes around again and repeated his question, Xiangjie pointed across the crowd and said loudly, "There, that bald-headed one, in the white vest — what are you prodding me for?" The last was addressed to eighty-one-year-old Liu Zexing who, to her surprise, was glaring at her with furious eyes, as though she had betrayed her own people to the enemy. Xiangjie had never known the old man's eyes to look so vicious. In an instant, however, he had turned away from her, shifted his position and was standing with an outwardly unruffled appearance.

"Now, don't you people know the voice of the well-to-do peasant and landlord when you hear it?" asked Zhang Da. "Don't you recognize him? Maybe some of you still feel sorry for him? Does he have the right to speak at a meeting like this? The district committee thought there'd be some bad elements spreading rumours and sabotaging in the opening of the new course. And I've guaranteed we have no such people in our village. Looks nice for us, doesn't it? A fellow like that daring to speak in public! Isn't he still under surveillance?"

"Take him away!" he ordered sharply.

Timidly and quietly, people began to disperse.

As Xiangjie was looking right and left for Little Stone, she saw Old Man Xing coming towards her. Still holding his tobacco pouch and looking very perturbed, he gazed at her in a way quite unlike himself. She felt they had drawn farther apart than ever. It was evidently because she had pointed out Liu Ersheng, the man who was supposed to be under surveillance.

"Where's your uncle?" asked Old Man Xing.

"I haven't seen him," she said calmly and decisively.

"Old brother!" Liu Zexing came up to them. "Now that Yu Village market is going to shift, we're in for it. And we'll pay for it with our legs, too!"

"It's not only the walking, you'll get the cold shoulder, going to an outside market!" Old Man Xing walked through the crowd with Liu Zexing, talking in a low voice. "How can a cadre not follow the mass line? That's something unheard of! Can they go ahead with the job in this high-handed way with everyone against it?"

"Didn't you hear what Zhang Da said just now?" said Liu Zexing. "This sort of thing is certainly known to the people above. So you've got to keep a check on your tongue!"

"The project in itself," he continued, "is splendid of course; in the past we looked forward to the course of the Shu River being altered, and it never happened. We never dreamt, though, that when it did change its course it would go through our fields and put an end to our market."

Listening to his old crony, Old Man Xing turned ashen. He felt as uneasy as one deserted by his companions. He looked at the people around with a diffident baffled expression, like a sentenced prisoner looking at the free, happy people hurrying along in the street. Xiangjie, too, grew pale, for she was now suddenly reminded of her open-air booth she depended on for a living. If the Yu Village market was really moved north, what was she going to do? She decided to consult Zhang Da.

As soon as they entered the village, Liu Zexing walked towards his solitary hut at the rear. Like the old rogue that he was, he knew the father and daughter were going to have it out and preferred to be out of the line of firing.

As soon as Old Man Xing and his daughter were back at her home, he began to complain. "The old devil!" he muttered. "Just as he's needed to give his opinion, he melts away, as though he's a stranger."

Xiangjie was silent, thinking.

"If the river is going to pass between the two villages," said Old Man Xing, looking at his daughter, "I won't be able to come and see you. How are you going to fend for yourself and your son?"

He expected to hear her pour forth her grief, tell of her helplessness without his support, and of the sufferings she would have to endure. He would be infinitely comforted and satisfied if she said, "Oh, dad, you must come, even if you have to make a detour of twenty *li*!" But, to his surprise, she said with an absent-minded air, "You don't need to worry about that! Even if you can't come, we can make a detour and come to see you."

Old Man Xing looked at her uncomprehendingly. What could she be thinking of? How placidly she talked! Who was behind her? How could she be so calm at the prospect of doing without him, her father?

"Very well, then!" The old man turned as if going to depart. "I'm glad to know you can get along on your own. I won't bother coming tomorrow."

"The new course isn't opened yet, is it? You'll come in for a bowl of hot bean milk, won't you?" said Xiangjie, smiling to pacify him.

But her words failed to produce the desired effect. The old man suddenly changed colour. "What! . . . What do you mean? . . . Do you think I come in order to drink your bean milk?" he burst out, his lips trembling, as if it were the greatest insult his daughter had hurled at him. Xiangjie fell back a step in fright. Without saying another word he stomped off in high dudgeon. Not knowing what had upset him, Xiangjie's first impulse was to run after him and explain. As she reached the door, however, she thought the better of it. It would, after all, give her a little peace if the old man were to cut down his calls in the future. In fact, it suddenly dawned upon her that the new course would remove the bondage which she had always been held by her parents. A great sense of relief, of freedom from restraint, came over her.

"That's exactly what I have been wanting!" she thought. She would now say goodbye to the listless days that had been her lot. She was weary of the scruffy appearance of her uncle, and wished she would never again see the hypocritical face and vicious eyes of old Liu Zexing. Thinking along these lines cheered her up. When Zhang Da came to see her a little later and praised her, she gained even more confidence. She knew she must break with those old people.

"You did right today. You've made a big stride politically," he said. "I'll come again when I have time."

"But tell me," she said softly. "How about my beancurd booth after the market moves north?"

"What? Are you still thinking of depending on the market for a living?" Zhang Da cried aloud. "But we're going to make a great success of agriculture here. Aren't you planning to join a mutual-aid team?"

"All right," she said submissively. "I'll have to depend on you cadres to fix it up for me."

"Don't worry, I'll fix it, I promise you," he said firmly. "I'll pop in again!"

That evening, Xiangjie's uncle came along as usual with his stool, and old Liu Zexing too, with a handful of tea. They all wondered why Old Man Xing hadn't turned up.

"My dad won't be coming tonight. Boil the water yourselves if you want tea," said Xiangjie coldly. Adding a few ladlefuls of water to the pot, she left the visitors to themselves and set out to see an army dependent and find out how she got along with Zhang Da's mutual-aid team.

The two old men did not stay long. "Maybe she's had a tiff with her father," said the ex horse-dealer as they were leaving. "I'm afraid the old man's losing control over his daughter."

"How do you mean?"

"Don't you know who pointed out Liu Ersheng today? Weren't you there?"

"Huh! We'll see how she gets along if she sets herself against her father!"

5

The next evening Xiangjie was due to grind the beans, but the old man was squatting on the *kang* smoking, when his wife came home after a meeting.

"What! Aren't you going to Yu Village?" she asked. Then she told him that in the meeting it was decided that a subsidy for removal would be paid to those whose ancestral graves lay within the new river course, that the owners of lands within the course would suggest how much compensation they should get, that this would be discussed and fixed collectively by the price-appraising group, and that an additional eighty catties of millet would be paid to the owner of every *mu* of wheat field. The old woman seemed quite satisfied, although they had neither ancestral graves nor land lying within the new course.

But the old man did not seem to hear her at all. "The good fortune of the land of Yu Village is done for," he muttered, heaving a sigh. "We are old," he turned to his wife, "if something happens to us, and word is sent to Yu Village, they'll have to go round by the Laohekou ferry. It's twenty *li* one way and forty there and back. She'll never be able to get here in time to see us in our last moments!"

"To my mind, the harvest is the big thing. If the river gives no more trouble, Xiangjie can take two crops a year off her plot, she'll do all right, and that's all I ask for. If she can come in time to bid us farewell when our time comes, it'll be nice; what does it matter if she can't? We'll be buried underground all the same."

Old Man Xing did not mention the squabble with his daughter. On the surface, he seemed to make light of it; but appearances are deceptive. When he met her in the Yu Village market, he pretended not to see her. He still set up his vegetable stall in front of her booth. He did not talk to her, but made more fuss of Little Stone than ever, buying him two pomegranates before the market closed. Although Xiangjie saw all this, she did not brood over it. She bustled about happily and talked of the benefits they would get from the change of course of the Shu River even in the presence of Old Man Xing.

She began to talk more and more enthusiastically about water conservancy. "This is one of the state plans for water conservancy! It's aimed at doing away with floods over fifteen million *mu* of land in the lower reaches of the river!" she said. "It's not as simple as you'd think. All our land here will be irrigated, you know." And again, "Just think how much grain will be harvested every year off fifteen million *mu*. Compared with this, the shifting of the Yu market is nothing." All this she would say to people, simulating the tone of Zhang Da, when she was drawing water from the well, washing clothes by the river, or digging vegetables for the pigs in her private plot, her dark eyes alight with self-confidence. But the moment she saw Zhang Da striding towards her in the presence of all, she would get so red in the face she dared not raise her head. The members of the militia threw significant glances in her direction, and the young women of Yu Village would whisper to one another when they saw her. Zhang Da's sweetheart, they called her. Liu Ying, the army dependent, once asked her softly over her shoulder, "When shall we drink toasts to your happiness?"

As a matter of fact, she and Zhang Da had not talked the matter over yet, but the open secret was corroborated by the looks of the girls who regarded the mutual affection between the two as their own triumph and a serious blow to the upholders of feudal tradition.

"Huh! If Xiangjie is willing, how dare her uncle stand in her way!"

"As soon as the new course is opened, Guan and Yu Villages will be separated. What can the old man do then? The couple can do whatever they like! He won't be able to come across from the other side."

All this talk came to Liu Si's ears, but he had no time to bother about it, for he and all the pedlars of Yu Village were busy finding out what sort of articles they could profitably sell after the work on the new course began. The peasants around Yu Village were making inquiries about who wanted to sell their land. The price of marshy land doubled overnight, yet no seller could be found.

It would take too long to describe the complex class struggle during the process of the project which took three years to complete. We shall therefore return to Old Man Xing and Xiangjie.

Zhang Da married Xiangjie as early as the spring of 1951 and their second son is now a year old. A farming co-op of seventy households was set up in Yu Village. The market was shifted ten *li* off, north of the village. The streets of Yu Village are now cleared of the earthen stoves and sticks used to erect the booths on market days. The spot where Xiangjie used to set up her beancurd stall is now a threshing ground. The stakes and bench legs were dislodged from the ground and sent to the co-op where you can still find them to this day lying in the livestock paddock. The yield of the land around Yu Village is threefold higher than before, for in the course of the project every household along the river stored up piles of beancake fertilizer. From afar, they looked like so many big hay stacks.

Every year Xiangjie pays two visits to Guan Village with her youngest, and on festival days Mama Xing comes to see her daughter, making a detour of Laohekou. The two of them, mother and daughter, are on very good terms. Old Man Xing still keeps aloof. But he is drawn to Little Stone, always asking the routine questions: "When are you going to be through primary school? How's old dad Liu Zexing? Does he ever ask after me?"

The old man is now doing odd-jobs in the co-op of Guan Village, peeling off corn-cobs with the women or stripping hemp husks. He also cuts grass for the animals and opens irrigation channels for the co-op fields. He checks in over seventy workdays in a year.

"Well, even if he could only earn sixty workdays, it wouldn't be so bad!" Mama Xing always says. "If I die one of these days, I know I can close my eyes in peace. For after all, the old man's got something to depend on."

Translated by Yu Fanqin and Zhang Zongzhi

Luo Binji was born in 1917 in Hui-chun County, Jilin Province, and began writing novels and short stories in the 1930s. He wrote A Brief Biography of Xiao Hong *in 1947. During the 1950s, he published several collections of his work reflecting pre- and post-Liberation China from a variety of perspectives.*

He is now a member of the national committee of the Federation of Literary and Art Circles, a member of the council of the Chinese Writers' Association, vice-chairman of its Beijing branch, and a member of the committee of the Sixth Beijing People's Political Consultative Conference.

The Girl Who Sold Wine

Xu Huaizhong

JIEDONG is a tiny market village near the Yunnan border. It's an out of the way place but the setting is lovely. Backed against a mountain, a river flowing at its feet, the village is surrounded by green groves of banana trees. In the morning, a thin mist rises from the river, as though someone in the heavens was pulling up a gossamer veil. On even days of the months there is a market fair, and Dai women, their bamboo baskets dangling from carrying-poles, go in groups. As they walk swaying more gracefully than the drifting mist, it's like a scene from another world.

At the entrance to the market street stands a large tree, beneath which women sell mulled wine. If you want something a bit superior, they'll put a couple of eggs in the mulling cauldron for you. In Jiedong, all the wine sellers are women. Formerly among them was a girl called Dao Hanmeng. There was nothing special about her — all Dai girls are pretty and well-formed.

But she seemed to be particularly attractive. Her stand was always crowded with customers, with others waiting behind to be served. It was as if her cauldron and bowls were magnetized. They drew people from scores of paces away.

Was Hanmeng's wine especially tasty? No. Did she give unusually good service? Far from it. She scarcely even looked at her customers, whoever they were. She had an air about her of "Drink if you like; if you don't, be off!" But her customers were all very patient. They would watch her quietly, and wait and wait. A late-comer might wait a long time and when it was finally his turn find that the mulling cauldron was empty. Yet instead of being displeased he always walked away looking quite satisfied.

Perhaps it was because she was the only wine seller who was still unmarried. They married young in that region. Hanmeng was no longer a little girl. Her body amply filled her form-fitting blouse and her long narrow skirt. But she remained single. Of course, every year a number of bold young fellows asked for her hand, but all were rebuffed. One or two even thought of staging a kidnap-marriage — it was still the custom in those parts — but they couldn't carry it off. If the girl herself was unwilling, neither heaven nor earth could move her. It ended with several young men constantly watching her, like a flock of hawks on high. But they only soared in circles above their quarry. None of them dared to swoop down.

Hanmeng's only close relative was her mother. They lived together in a lone bamboo house outside the village. When Hanmeng was nine, her mother became paralysed and was unable to leave her bed ever since. Hanmeng had to take her place as a wine seller. Now many years had passed and much had happened. But Hanmeng's life was like a still pool, with never a ripple. She was accustomed to being alone, and to being lonely. Dai girls like to sing and dance. But no one ever saw

Hanmeng do either. She never even touched a mouth harp. Hanmeng showed no interest in anything. It was as if she heard nothing, saw nothing, of what was going on around her. Nor did she have any hopes or aspirations. Except for looking after her mother, she silently made her wine, and silently sold it in the market-place. She was completely unconcerned with the fact that she was already twenty-one.

Now, let me tell you about another person.

In Jiedong there was a medical team that gave free treatment. It consisted of a young acting physician and two nurses. Yunnan had only recently been liberated, and there was a great need for cadres in all parts of the province. For the time being it wasn't possible to provide a remote place like Jiedong with all the staff it needed. Zhao Chiming, the acting physician, had been discharged from the army not long before, where he had served as a medical orderly. He had no other special training. But in the village he was considered simply a wonder. People sent for him in every part of Jiedong and on both sides of the river. If some mother's milk suddenly dried up, she sought Zhao. If a water buffalo quit eating grass, Zhao was the man consulted.

As he rushed around, making his calls, he was frequently heard to groan: "This sort of thing is miles out of my line! Why do they have to ask me?"

But if they didn't ask Zhao, whom could they ask? Except for him the only other one they could seek a cure from was the idol in the temple. Not only did the local people worship Zhao as omnipotent, they considered him a dear and close friend. Any family that had a marriage was sure to invite Zhao to the feast. When a husband and wife quarrelled, Zhao was always the one

they asked to mediate. Whenever he passed, young and
old poked their heads out of their windows and called:
"Dr Zhao, come in and sit a while!" And if it was meal-
time, they insisted on dragging him in and making him
eat his fill.

Every Sunday the young acting physician went to the
wine stands beneath the big tree to inspect. When the
women saw him coming they hurriedly wiped their
bowls and spoons and shooed off the flies. Plainly, they
were a little afraid of him. Not that he had a bad
temper. But he frequently, right in front of their customers, criticized them for this or that being too dirty.
And he often lectured the customers on the danger of
flies. To hear him talk you'd think that after one portion of mulled wine from an unclean bowl you were
sure to collapse.

But Hanmeng didn't care about Zhao's inspections.
Nothing could drive her customers away. Once, when
Zhao picked up a dirty bowl from her stand, she took it
from him without a word, filled it with wine and held
it out before her customers. Several hands immediately
snatched for it.

One day, Zhao came again to the big tree. He discovered that the place where Hanmeng usually set up
her stand was empty. In spite of himself, he felt reliev-
ed. To tell the truth, that Hanmeng was hard to handle.
But as he turned to leave, his mind was troubled. Why?
He admitted to himself it was because he wanted to
know why Hanmeng hadn't appeared. He asked several
of the other wine sellers about her, but none of them
knew. So Zhao walked away. But a few minutes later,
when he looked around, he saw through a grove of
papaya trees a small lone bamboo house. It was Han-

meng's home. How had he come to this place? Oh well, since he was here, he might as well go in and have a look.

When he pushed open the door, he was met with a foul stuffy odour. Hanmeng was lying on a sleeping mat on the floor, her face burning with fever, her lips dry and blistered. She was obviously in pain. Her mother reclined at her side, tears in her eyes.

Under the circumstances how could the acting physician hold back? He quickly took his stethoscope out of his instruments case — he carried it with him wherever he went. To his surprise the two women glared at him. In their eyes he could see fear, caution and hostility. When he tried to approach her, Hanmeng pushed herself up to a sitting position and demanded coldly:

"What do you want? What are you trying to do?"

And the mother added: "Go, I beg you, go at once. We don't need pity from anyone."

The fact was that both mother and daughter hated doctors. It was because of something that happened when Hanmeng was still a baby. Papa was very ill. Mama went to the temple and prayed to the gods. She spent a lot of money in contributions, but the sick man didn't get any better. Just at that time a quack medicine pedlar, a Han, set up a canopy on the street and laid out his medicines. He claimed to be able to cure anything. Mama invited him to the house. He took the sick man's pulse, then shook his head and said: "Start preparing for the funeral."

Mama wept and pleaded. Finally the faker said he would try. Mama had him move in, so that he could cope with any emergency. He lived with them for near-

The Girl Who Sold Wine 125

ly a month.   His travelling case was lightened by a few
ampoules of medicine, but it was filled with money —
money that represented the family's savings over the
years and their only plot of rice paddy land.   When the
condition of the invalid became really critical, the
"doctor" suddenly disappeared, together with his port-
able medicine case.

Zhao didn't understand why he was being treated in
such an unfriendly manner, but there was no time to
talk.   He went back and brought the two nurses and
forced the girl to submit to an examination.   She was
suffering from malignant malaria. . . .   What followed,
you can imagine.   The physician did his utmost to
save her.   In order to give her the best possible care,
at night he slept in a little ante-room where the mother
usually chanted her prayers.   Separated from the sick
girl by only a thin partition, he could hear her breathing
clearly.   She had only to utter the slightest groan and
he rose immediately to look after her.   He often sat up
with her half the night; his eyes grew as red as ripe
peaches from loss of sleep.   His superiors had decided
to send him back to the provincial capital for special
medical studies and his replacement had already arrived.   But Zhao didn't leave until he was convinced that
Hanmeng was well on the way to recovery.

Two years later, Zhao returned to Jiedong.   The
health department had sent out a group to investigate
areas where malignant malaria was endemic — Jiedong
had been just such an area for years — and since Zhao
knew the local situation, his studies were temporarily
interrupted and he was assigned to the group.

It used to take a month from the provincial capital

to the more remote areas near the border, because you had to go on horseback. Now a highway had been built, and you could do it by bus in four days. But the last twenty kilometres to Jiedong through the difficult mountain terrain had not yet been completed, so the group spent the night with some Jingpo people living at the road terminus, intending to finish the journey on foot the next day. The hospitable Jingpos entertained them cordially, tidying up their houses and vying for the privilege of providing them with sleeping quarters.

In the home where Zhao stayed, the wife had just given birth a few days before and was still in bed. When she heard that the team was going to Jiedong, she had her husband give a small package of delicacies to Zhao with the request that he deliver it to Dr Li Shuhui in the Jiedong hospital. The Jingpo people spoke of this woman doctor with obvious respect and affection. The husband told Zhao the following story:

His wife had been in labour for a day and a night. Though in great pain, she could not give birth. When the local garrison learned of this, they telephoned to the village across the river, where a visiting medical team from the Jiedong hospital happened to have arrived the day before. Dr Li, leader of the team, promised to come at once. But a long time passed, and she still did not appear. Carrying his umbrella, the husband decided to go to the village to urge her to hurry. When he got to the river, he found it enormously swollen from the rains of the previous night. It was quite impassable. Usually the river was practically dry; you could cross it in almost a single stride. But when a flash flood roared down from the mountains, the two sides were completely cut off.

What to do! Nearly wild with anxiety, he paced to and fro along the shore. Suddenly, he saw the waves pushing something towards the bank. It was a woman. Pale, her hair soaking in the water, she was holding on to a bamboo door with both arms. The door had been nearly battered to pieces by the waves, and was held together only by two boards which were bound to it tightly.

Luckily, she was driven into a cove near the shore. Otherwise, that would have been the end of her. He rushed down and dragged her out. Attached to her waist was a packet bound in several thicknesses of oilcloth. Opening it, he found a small box marked with a red cross. The husband couldn't restrain a shout of joy. This woman must be the leader of the medical team. He carried her to his house on his back.

After a while, she revived. When she saw the Jingpo people standing around her, for the moment she didn't know where she was. She asked questions with difficulty, her lips trembling. But they understood her meaning and explained that she was in the house of the woman in labour. She rose immediately, though she nearly fell — she was so weak. But she set to work without a word. An hour later the babies were born. They were twins — a pair of boys!

The neighbours present were overjoyed. And as for the parents — well, you can just imagine. The woman who had assisted the delivery seemed more excited than any of them. Holding one baby in each arm she looked as if she wanted to raise them to the sky. She knew that a difficult birth could mean the end of both mother and child. Today she had saved not only two lives, but three! Why shouldn't she be excited?

But once the tension was over, she could sustain herself no longer, and collapsed in a faint. It was only then that people observed that her body was a mass of bruises.

Zhao was very stirred by the husband's story. Firstly, he knew that Jiedong now had a hospital, something he had been hoping for two years ago. Secondly, he was proud of his colleague, the woman leader of the medical team. He told the husband he would be delighted to deliver the package to Dr Li personally.

When the malaria inspection group arrived in Jiedong, virtually the whole hospital staff turned out to welcome them. The first one to shake Zhao's hand was a woman doctor. "Are you Dr Li?" he asked. When she said that she was, Zhao looked the young doctor over once more and again shook her hand. Then he gave her the gift package. She looked puzzled. "A Jingpo family has sent this to you," Zhao explained, "for delivering their twins. They said they're coming to see you in a few days."

Dr Li laughed. "Not me. They've made a mistake."

What had happened was this: Dr Li was giving a sick girl an injection when a telephone call came from across the river saying that a Jingpo woman was having a difficult delivery. Since that was the case, Dr Li would have to go personally, and very soon. But unexpectedly the girl she was treating got worse. Dr Li couldn't leave her. Just then one of the midwives asked that she be allowed to go. She was a new trainee, and had never handled a difficult birth alone. But all the other midwives were out, so Dr Li had to agree. The river flooded that day and the midwife had to swim across, clinging to a bamboo door. It was very dangerous. She nearly went down in the rolling waves. But she got across and made the delivery. Then she fainted, and was in a dazed condition all night. The following day, the river subsided. She was brought back to the hospital in Jiedong on a cart delivering grain from the garrison. It wasn't until the following day that she completely recovered.

Returning the gift packet to Zhao, Dr Li suggested: "You'd better give this to our midwife." She called a nurse over and said: "Take this comrade to Dao Han-meng."

Oho! So it was she! Zhao was amazed. A while ago, when he was passing the big tree, he had thought of looking to see how his patient Hanmeng was getting on. Now he reproached himself. Why should he have thought that she would always remain a wine seller?

The fact was that after Hanmeng recovered from malaria she went to the hospital and asked that they let her work there. She was willing to sweep the floors, cook, wash clothes. When she was sick she had used a lot of medicine, but she had no money. She wanted to pay for it by her work. Dr Li, the hospital chief, only laughed, and said that the people were entitled to free medical services. Later, when the hospital started a training course for midwives, Dr Li remembered Han-meng, and went to call on her and invited her to take part. Although Hanmeng wasn't very clear what the course was all about, she readily consented. They saved my life, she thought. It's only right that I should do something for them.

Hanmeng learned to assist deliveries, but that wasn't the most important thing she learned. At the same time she came to understand something she had never understood before. Take Comrade Zhao, the young acting physician for example. He was of the Han race, far from home and dear ones. He had come to Jiedong like a man dropped out of the sky. Wherever someone was ill, there he went, through wind and rain, day or night, never complaining of hardship or fatigue, never fearing that the evil spirit possessing the ill person would attach itself to him. And he never got anything for it. Why did he do it? What did he want? However you looked at it, there was nothing in it for him.

But now Hanmeng understood. Zhao had no selfish reason. He didn't want anything. He was just that kind of a person. She herself didn't know when she started, but Hanmeng often found herself staring off into space with her lustrous eyes. She tried to remember what Zhao looked like, but her recollection of him was vague. She couldn't recall what he wore; she wasn't even sure about his face. She had never really paid much attention to him before. After she fell ill, they were frequently together, but that was at a time when her mind was hazy. She had one impression, however, that was very strong — how large and cool his hand was each time he put it on her forehead, and how, when he removed his hand, he always, in the same motion, smoothed the hair at her temples.

Recalling this, Hanmeng's heart beat fast. She thought and thought. A whole series of pictures formed in her mind — beautiful, imaginary pictures. They say that people who don't like to talk are fond of dreaming. That's absolutely true.

She remembered that when he left Jiedong he didn't say a word to her. Now two years had gone by with never a message or letter. How she longed to see him.

But she would never see him again. He was like a meteor that streaked across the sky, seeming to open its arms to you wide. But when you wanted to get another glimpse of it, it was gone for good.

To get back to Zhao — he should have remained with the inspection group authorities while they chatted with Dr Li in the hospital reception room. But instead he excused himself, saying he had to deliver something that had been entrusted to him. Then he went out with the nurse to find Hanmeng.

The nurse brought him to a new building. It was a primary school, and classes were in session. Why had they come here, Zhao wondered. The nurse pointed through one of the windows. Seated in the last row was a woman dressed in the tight fitting blouse of the Dai people, but wearing a cloth cap over her short-cropped hair. Was she the teacher? No. She obviously was listening to the lesson. Could she be a student? She didn't look like one. She was much bigger and older than the others in the class. When she happened to turn her face in his direction, Zhao finally recognized her. It was Hanmeng.

Perhaps it wasn't proper for such a grown-up person to sit on a bench in a classroom with a lot of children. But that didn't bother Hanmeng. She came to the school whenever she had time, quietly slipping in, and quietly sitting down in the last row. Although she couldn't keep up with the other students because she was not able to attend every class, her interest in no way diminished. She had secretly sworn to herself that she would not live in vain, that she would become a useful person. Best of all would be if she could become an acting physician — the same kind as Zhao. She knew that achieving this would be much harder than selling wine. She would have to study intently. And since by sitting with the children she could learn to read, and do mathematics, and even understand many things about the stars in the sky, why shouldn't she come to school?

The nurse wanted to knock on the door and call Hanmeng out. But Zhao wouldn't permit it. He stood waiting by the window until the bell rang dismissing the class. When Hanmeng emerged, Zhao walked forward to meet her. She was so surprised to see him that she automatically fell back a step. It was too sudden, too unexpected. Flurried, frightened, for several moments she couldn't speak. Finally, gazing at him unbelievingly with her big lustrous eyes, she said shyly: "You've returned. . . ."

They left the school yard together. Zhao had forgotten completely the packet he was supposed to deliver. Holding it in his hand, he walked shoulder to shoulder with Hanmeng to the street. When they reached a quiet spot, Hanmeng asked softly: "Why didn't you say anything the day you left?"

"I went to your house," Zhao replied in a low voice, "but you were asleep. I wanted to awaken you, but I thought — what can I say? I didn't know, so I let you sleep."

As they talked, they followed a small path deep into a banana grove. Except for the droning of cicadas all was still. How quiet it was. Only then did they realize that they were wandering aimlessly. And so they halted. Hanmeng lowered her head and covered her burning cheeks with her hands.

"Come," she said. "Let's go home. I'll have mama make you some mulled wine."

February 1958

Translated by Sidney Shapiro

 *Xu Huaizhong was born in 1929 in Handan County, Hebei Province. Since 1953, he has published the novella* Rainbow over the Earth *and written numerous poems, stories and songs. His major works are the novel* On the Tibetan Highlands *and the short story* Anecdotes from the Western Front, *which won a national short story award in 1980.*

He joined the Chinese Writers' Association in 1956 and is now a scriptwriter with the August First Film Studio.

An Ordinary Labourer

Wang Yuanjian

GENERAL Lin and Colonel Liu got down from the bus, took the towel cloths from their necks and mopped their perspiring faces. Then they shouldered their bundles and hastened along the road towards the construction site.

Originally, they had planned to reach camp early, and go with their unit when it marched off to begin its two to ten shift. But the conference they had attended that morning had lasted longer than they expected. To make matters worse, their bus broke down on the road and was half an hour late; it didn't arrive at the camp until after three in the afternoon. Instead of getting off, they bought tickets to the next stop, which was nearer the dam.

"We've missed class," quipped the general. "Better hurry and do some make-up work or we'll be left behind."

The mid-June weather was at its hottest in late afternoon. Powdery dust rose from every step on the scorched dirt road. The atmosphere was oppressive, charged; you had the feeling that you had only to strike a match and the air would burst into flame.

Supporting the bundle on his shoulder with one hand,

in his other hand the general held a string bag containing his wash basin and other toilet articles. He walked with large strides. Even before they entered the valley, sweat had soaked through the back of his tunic. Beads of perspiration dripped from his greying temples beneath his wide-brimmed straw hat.

Colonel Liu, who had been trudging behind him, hurried a few steps to catch up. Panting, he proffered the small package in his hand and said, "Let me take that bundle, general. You take this. It's not so heavy."

"Forget it. You're no youngster either." The general looked at Colonel Liu and smiled. "We two are about the same."

The colonel was really having a difficult time. Not only was he ageing, but he was quite stout. The heat was hard on him. The upper half of his body looked as if it had been boiled. Sweat was streaming down his cheeks.

"Perhaps you'd like to rest a while?" Colonel Liu suggested hopefully.

"Not necessary. I'll shift this bundle and I'll be fine." The general halted, removed the grey tunic, faded almost white with many washings, and hung it over his arm. Beneath, he wore only a sleeveless undershirt. He raised the bundle to his other shoulder and hailed a passing comrade.

"How far to the dam site?"

"It's just ahead." The man pointed to a wooden arch.

Sure enough, stepping through the archway, they were greeted with the hum of voices and machinery, and the blare of loudspeakers. The whole panorama of the dam site unrolled before them. It was huge. A long earthen dam was rising upon the valley floor to link two mountains at either end. Conveyer belts, like endless pythons, carried earth and gravel up the slope of the dam. Atop the dam and at its base, people, trucks, bulldozers swarmed in continuous rapid motion. . . .

The general was stirred. He knew this place well. Nine years before he had wracked his brains here, helping prepare the campaign to capture and hold these mountains with their tombs of the ancient Ming emperors. More than once he had pored over battle maps of the area, and peered at every peak through his field glasses. To this day he still remembered the exact altitude of each.

But the old battlefield was completely changed. The enemy fortifications were long since gone. Where a small branch of the Great Wall had been was only a white scar on the mountains. Even the little hill in the valley was now half its original size; its whole upper section had been removed and incorporated into the dam.

Whenever he saw construction going on in a place where he had fought or camped the general always felt a certain warmth, a kind of sweetness. Coming back to the Ming Tombs region today as an ordinary labourer, he experienced these emotions even more intently. His discomfort and weariness were completely forgotten.

The general and the colonel walked until they found a sign bearing the unit designation of the section they were to join. They had chosen this particular unit because working here they could get to know men with whom they usually had little contact.

Everyone was very busy. At the foot of a metre high ramp were a string of tip-cars on a small gauge railway.

The People's Liberation Army men in this section were
divided into three teams. One team filled the baskets
with earth and gravel; another carried the baskets a
distance of about thirty metres and mounted a ramp;
a third dumped the baskets into the tip-cars.

Like an embarrassed tardy pupil, the general pulled
the colonel to one side, and they quietly deposited their
luggage. Then, adjusting their wide straw hats, they
entered the section. They searched for tools for several
minutes, but in vain. Finally, they discovered two
empty wicker baskets. They each took one, and used it
to carry earth, by hand.

This method proved to be quite awkward. It was
slow, inefficient and hurt the hands. So as not to hold
up others, they left the board walks and tramped
through the sand. The general had made several trips
from the basket-fillers to the top of the ramp when a
bright, high-pitched voice hailed him.

"Hey, old comrade, how come you're going it alone?
Don't you like team work?"

The friendly teasing brought a smile to the general's
face. He looked around. The speaker was a round-
faced young soldier of about twenty. He had a faint
suggestion of down on his upper lip. The lock of hair
protruding from under the peak of his cap was plastered
by perspiration to his forehead. He was the picture of
mischief. Toting two earth-filled baskets on the ends
of a shoulder pole, he walked towards the general with
a rhythmic gait. Grinning impishly, he revealed clean
white teeth.

The general laughed. "I'm a new recruit!"

"Wait a minute." The boy deftly dumped the earth
from his baskets, then ran and fetched a large deep

basket from behind one of the gravel screens. Placing it down before the general, he said:

"Let's form a 'mutual-aid team' with this. What do you say?"

"Good," replied the general. He squatted and helped the boy remove the two shallow baskets and affix the suspension rope of the big basket to the centre of the carrying pole.

Tightening the knots, the boy glanced at the general disapprovingly. "You won't do at all," he said in the critical voice of an old veteran. "You can't go around in just an undershirt the first day. You'll get a bad burn in this hot sun." After the general put on his tunic, the boy continued to impart the benefit of his experience.

"Drink plenty of water," he said. "And, in a little while, when the pickled vegetables come, eat a lot. At the end of the shift, be sure to empty all the sand from your shoes, or you'll raise blisters on the march back to camp. Wash your hands and feet in hot water before going to bed. We have very good conditions here. Every man gets two ladlesful of hot water. . . ."

Gazing gratefully at the boy's face, the general agreed to each of his recommendations. He liked this youngster very much. They began to chat. He learned that the boy's name was Li Shouming, that he was in a messenger squad and was twenty-one years of age. Li Shouming had joined the army in 1955; plainly he considered himself a veteran. The general learned a good deal from him about work here and conditions in his unit.

Chatting easily, by the time the big basket was tied to the pole, the two were old friends. The general affectionately called the boy "Young Li". And Young Li familiarly addressed the comrade in the faded grey tunic as "Old Lin".

They carried the basket to the gravel pit, where the shovellers filled it to the brim. Not satisfied, the general added a "steamed muffin" — piling in more gravel and sand to form a rounded top. This brought on his first argument with Young Li. As the general was crouching to get his shoulder under the front end of the carrying pole, Young Li pulled the rope knot half a foot along the pole towards himself. The general saw him.

"You mustn't do that," the general said reprovingly, moving the knot back to the centre.

"I'm strong. A little extra weight won't hurt me." Young Li again pulled the knot towards his end.

"You're cheating because I can't see behind me." The general moved the knot forward. "Our total ages come to over 70, and mine is more than two-thirds of that number. The weight belongs on my side!"

Young Li was stumped.

The first argument was settled. But after two trips, another one arose. Young Li began it.

"This way is no good. You're not nimble enough. It's not safe. You're liable to trip over those baskets waiting to be dumped, and hurt yourself."

"It doesn't matter."

"Doesn't matter?" Young Li shifted to another point of attack. "Besides, you walk too slowly. You can't be our 'locomotive'. We hold up the teams behind us."

This time the general was stumped. It was true, because of old wounds in his side and legs, he couldn't walk very quickly.

"Come on, Old Lin, you handle the rudder. I'll take the prow."

Young Li finally triumphed.

In spite of their arguments, the two co-operated extremely well. With Young Li in the lead and the general counting cadence, they walked in an even, matched pace. They shared the same piece of salted turnip, they drank from the same canteen. With each trip they made up the ramp, they felt this friendship "that forgot age" growing closer and firmer.

And each time they came down the ramp with emptied baskets, Young Li gazed respectfully at the white rime of dried perspiration that formed a line on the general's greying hair along the rim of his straw hat. The old comrade certainly has a lot of drive, Young Li thought to himself. He must know that shovelling is easier, but he insists on carrying this heavy basket. . . .

The general was becoming very fond of the young soldier. On the back of his yellow sleeveless shirt was a big "5", and the boy carried earth with the same flowing restlessness he undoubtedly displayed on the athletic field. For instance, when you brought your basket to the top of ramp, all you had to do was put it down behind the others and wait for it to be emptied. But Young Li always delivered theirs right to the very edge — to "make it easier for them to load the tip-cars".

And on the way down, he was always shouting orders and gesticulating. Or he grumbled and moved the baskets of those who hadn't put them in their proper places. He invariably carried back a few more empty baskets, in addition to his own. He had many criticisms. Either the car-loaders were too few — they were holding up the work. Or he would shout: "Watch how you fling those empty baskets. You're liable to hurt someone!"

The general found the boy's criticisms in complete accord with what he was thinking himself. He was learning to understand Young Li better with every trip they made. The general paid frequent visits to the lower ranks. Only the other day he had worked in his "experimental plot" — one of the companies. And he often chatted with the soldiers. But although he had used these methods for the past several years, they never gave him the comprehension of the average soldier's thinking and emotions which he got working together these few hours with Young Li. The boy's attitude of being one of the masters of his own society, his striving to do well, his sense of collectiveness.... The general linked these with his "experimental plot" company, with his own work.... He became so immersed in his contemplations that several times he nearly stumbled.

Pondering, working, the general was surprised to discover that three hours had flown by.

At six-thirty, two cooks arrived with a large basket of steamed muffins and a pail of pickled vegetables. The tip-cars rolled off with their load and did not return. Evidently the men at the other end of the line were eating. Everyone promptly swarmed around the muffin hamper. The general squeezed his way through the cheerful crowd and took two muffins and two pieces of pickled turnip. Then he found a sand dune and sat down.

It was only then that he realized how tired he was. Not that hard work was new to him. By 1930, he had already put in three years pulverizing and carrying ore in a mine. And, of course, there were the long difficult years in the Red Army. But that was all years ago. Today, three hours of hauling sand and gravel brought home to him that he was not as strong as he used to be. The sun made him dizzy. His shoulders were red and swollen from the carrying pole. His back and legs were stiff, and the old wound in his side was beginning to hurt. A bullet had fractured one of his ribs when they were fighting the reactionary troops in 1935.

The general rolled over and let the hot sand bake his wounded side. The warmth was very comforting. He took a bite of muffin and lightly drummed his stiff legs with his fist. It doesn't matter, he said to himself. If I can stick it out today, tomorrow won't be any problem.

Lolling against the sand dune, he munched his muffin and gazed at the dam. Black rain clouds were racing from behind the mountain ridge and piling up over the construction site. Against the dark, heaving background, the dam looked like a battleship, floating majestically through stormy seas. Bursting dynamite, like volleys from artillery batteries, on the mountains at either end, sent smoke and dust sailing into the heavens. As if borrowing the booming explosions for rhythmic accompaniment, the loudspeakers were transmitting the brave strains of the popular song:

I'm a soldier, and I come from good plain stock.
Revolutionary battles have steeled me....

The scene made the general very happy. A heavy voice drifted over from the other side of the sand dune. Someone was telling a story:

"... That was what you call hard work. Earth, timber, timber, earth, all day long. No comfortable eight-hour shifts for us. We just kept at it...."

"And did you get them done in time?" another voice asked tensely.

"Of course. Our divisional commander came and

wielded a shovel right with us. How could we fail!
The division C.O. and I shouldered a log together. He
carried the front end. As we walked, Commander Lin
called: 'Let's finish building these fortifications quickly,
comrades! Make them so tight that the enemy won't
even be able to get a drop of water through!' He certainly knew how to put things!...'' The heavy voice
paused. There was the sound of crunching pickled
turnip, then the voice resumed:

"Now that's the way we've got to build this dam —
so that not a drop of water can get through! It seems
to me —'' A roar of laughter drowned out the rest.

General Lin smiled. He knew the engagement the
man was talking about. Whether he had actually said
those words, he didn't really remember, but they recalled to him the tense atmosphere of the time. He
automatically looked at the big earthen dam again.
He's right, the general thought. There are many simi-
larities between those days and now.

The general was about to get up and take a look at
the speaker, when a spray of sand dropped by his side.
Young Li was coming towards him in leaps and bounds.

"So this is where you are. I've been searching everywhere.'' Young Li offered him a straw hat full of muffins. The boy took a swig from his canteen, then handed that to the general too.

The general drank, and asked, "Have you been looking for me long?''

"No. When I couldn't find you, I went to listen to
our section chief tell a story.''

"Ah.'' The general gazed affectionately at the boy's
perspiring face. He handed Young Li his towel cloth
and slightly shook his head. "Just look at you. This

work is tiring enough without you dashing all over the place during the break."

"There's nothing to this job," Young Li replied excitedly, mopping his face. "We're doing a little work, but we've got tents to live in and we eat steamed muffins made of pure white flour. You call that tiring? The way the old Red Army climbed the Snowy Mountains and crossed the marshlands on the Long March — now that was *really* hard." He took a bite of muffin and asked the general, "Have you heard the stories of the Red Army on the Long March, Old Lin?"

The general smiled, but did not reply.

"You haven't? I've heard lots of them." The boy grew animated. He forgot the muffin in his hand. "Our political instructor told us. The Long March was very difficult. When the Red Army crossed the marshlands, they ran out of food. They ate grass roots and wild herbs. One comrade was so hungry, he boiled his leather belt and finished it off in one day."

Obviously, the youngster was embroidering the story. You couldn't eat tough leather belts like crisp cucumber. It had taken the general three full days in the marshlands to consume his leather sole. But, infected by the boy's ardour, he didn't bother to correct him. He only remarked, "Under those circumstances, what else could you do?" At the time, eating leather belts and soles had seemed to him entirely natural.

"What!" The old comrade's mild response aroused the boy's anger. Red in the face, he sputtered, "You-you-you don't have the least idea what our old revolutionaries went through!" He rolled over and lay with his hands pillowed beneath his head, furious, clearly determined to say no more to this unfeeling individual.

"Our old revolutionaries," he muttered, "so many gave their lives, they suffered so. Now they hand the country they won over to us and say, 'Do a good job of construction. Let everybody work and everybody enjoy the benefits!' If we don't do this right, how will we be able to look them in the eye? . . ."

The general turned and glanced at the boy's agitated face. A warm, tender feeling stole over him. Although Young Li wasn't fully clear about the nature of his responsibilities, through him the general could see one thing plainly: The glorious tradition of hard life and bitter struggle of the older generation of fighters had already been accepted as a precious heritage by the younger generation. This heritage educated them and inspired them to devote themselves to building socialism; under new conditions it was bursting forth into new blazing flowers.

Moved, the general said, "Recalling those times makes us want to work with greater drive than ever today!"

"Now you're talking sense." Young Li seemed a bit mollified. He ate his muffin, and leaned close and whispered in the older man's ear, "Our generals are the ones who really work hard. Have you ever seen them work?"

The general only laughed.

"Don't you believe me? I saw one once." Young Li sat up abruptly and said in a confidential voice, "One night at three o'clock in the morning I was called up out of bed and given an urgent message to deliver to a general — our political commissar. I thought: He must be asleep. But what do you think?" The boy paused, then said with unconcealed admiration, "He was writing at his desk!"

"Generals have to work too. Wasn't it the same for you? You had to get up in the middle of the night."

"There you go again!" Young Li retorted in annoyance. "I had a couple of hours' sleep already — he was working right along!..." Before he could say more, a big drop of rain struck his cheek. A wild gritty wind swooped down and rain fell in heavy white sheets, the drops raising little smoky puffs as they struck the powdery soil.

The storm was sudden and fierce. Men ran about looking for their raincapes and seeking shelter. In an instant, every place that offered some protection from the wind — the pits, behind the gravel screens, behind the sand dunes — was crowded with people. Young Li looked at the railway tracks and saw that the tip-cars had not yet returned. He pulled the general to his feet and led him in a short dash to a wooden lean-to. There they crouched, out of the storm.

The rain grew heavier, the wind blew harder. Someone had lost something and was shouting inquiries. Someone's straw hat went tumbling across the diggings like a runaway kite. Just at that time a wheeled tractor with a train of empty tip-cars, twisting and undulating like some legless centipede, came rumbling back to the loading place beside the ramp.

The comrades at the dam must be waiting, thought the general. We ought to load those cars. But the rain is so heavy.... Only a few comrades came out from their shelters and walked towards the ramp. But when the others didn't follow, they hesitated, and started to turn back. Young Li was bursting with impatience.

"Section chief! Section chief!" he shouted.

"The section chief has gone to a meeting!" someone replied.

The scene evoked a responsive chord in the general. This sort of thing often happened in battle. Everyone would know what ought to be done in a certain situation, and would be itching to do it. But because no one took the lead, an entire unit would remain immobile. At such a time, if someone said only one word the unit would immediately plunge into action. The general shook the boy's arm.

"Come on, Young Li. Let's go to work!"

"Right! But the section chief isn't here...."

"We'll start anyway!" The general put his hand on the boy's shoulder and pushed himself to his feet. Then he pulled Young Li up.

"Comrades," he shouted. "Let's go!"

He came out of the lean-to and advanced, crouching, into the gale.

His cry was like a command. Everyone stood up. Two, then three more ... came trotting out into the rain. Laughing, shouting, they followed the general towards the ramp. Some dashed on ahead of him. As he ran, the general glanced behind him. How many years is it since I've done this? he asked himself.

He was reminded of that day in the marshlands. They were also caught in a sudden rainstorm at dusk. Weak from cold and fatigue and hunger, the men had hurried towards a grove. He knew that if they didn't find drier ground to camp for the night, they would have to grope in the dark across treacherous marshes filled with bogs and quicksands. Then too he had called to his soldiers. Then too, responding, they had pushed on through the storm.

The general and Young Li were soaked to the skin by the time they reached the gravel pit. The gale flung raindrops and sand stinging against their faces. But they had no time for such matters. Seizing shovels, they energetically filled a large basket, shouldered the pole and hurried towards the ramp. Two men came running to meet them. The man in the lead grabbed the end of the pole which the general was supporting as the "rudder".

"Commander. . . ." he panted. Young Li couldn't hear him in the howling wind.

Peering at him, the general saw the red tabs on his shoulders. Behind him was Colonel Liu. Firmly, the general pushed the man's hand aside.

"I'm just a soldier here. You're the commander. . . . Comrade Section Chief, I have a suggestion. You'd better hurry and get things organized. It's hard to see in this storm. We ought to take special safety precautions!"

"Right." The section chief helplessly released the pole. "There was a meeting up at division. I just got back. . . ." he explained lamely. Then he hurried up to Young Li at the pole's front end.

Grasping the boy by the shoulder, he pulled him to a stop and said in a low voice. "The general's getting on in years, and he's been wounded. You must take good care of him. . . ."

"General!" cried the startled Young Li. His heart began to beat fast; he didn't know whether it was because he was moved or tense. Rain seemed to have got into his eyes: they smarted. Hastily, he lowered his end of the pole and turned to face the general.

June 29, 1958

Translated by Wen Xue

Wang Yuanjian was born in 1929 in Zhucheng County, Shandong Province. He joined the Eighth Route Army in 1944 and subsequently became a newspaper editor and correspondent for Xinhua News Agency. In 1952 he helped edit A Single Spark Can Start a Prairie Fire, *a collection of reminiscences of revolution, and from 1954 onwards published numerous short stories, including the anthologies* Party Membership Dues, An Ordinary Labourer *and* An Invaluable Memento. *He is now a scriptwriter with the August First Film Studio.*

My First Superior

Ma Feng

SOON after I graduated from the provincial Water Conservancy School last summer I was assigned to work in this county. I was in quite a state at the time — I don't know whether it was from excitement or tension. Probably all students feel the same way when they go to their first job.

With my luggage strapped to my bicycle, I rode off to "take office". I didn't travel by bus because I wanted to start training immediately for long trips by bike. I imagined I would need that ability, working in the countryside.

I set out before daybreak and it was nearly noon by the time I reached the county seat. No sooner had I entered town than I had an accident. The streets were rather narrow and as I pedalled along I saw an old man coming towards me. He looked a bit odd. Although it was the hottest part of summer, he wore a lined jacket and black cotton-padded trousers tied at the cuffs. His head was covered by a big straw hat. Was he avoiding the heat, or was he afraid of being cold?

Head down, back bent, hands clasped behind him, he advanced with a stately gait, his toes pointing outwards. I rang my bell loudly, but he didn't even raise his head. He just kept ambling along at the same deliberate pace. When we were only a few feet apart, he suddenly looked up and moved two steps to the right.

But it was too late. When I thought that he wasn't giving way, I cut right to pass him just as he was stepping in the same direction to avoid me and knocked him down. I fell too. Tired and hungry, I had been irritated by his hogging the road. Now my tumble made me furious. I crawled to my feet and picked up the bike.

"Are you deaf or something!" I shouted. "Didn't you hear my bell?"

I felt ashamed as soon as the words left my mouth. He hadn't refused to get out of the way; he had only been a little slow. What's more, I had run him down. Of course, he must be pretty annoyed. I was sure he wasn't going to let me get away with it; I was probably in for a row.

He picked up his hat and rose slowly. Much to my surprise he said calmly, "Don't lose your temper and I won't either. We've both had a fall, now let's go our separate ways."

This time I got a good look at him. He wasn't an old man at all. He couldn't have been more than forty. His square face was pale, his hair cropped short. He stood up, glanced at me, and brushed the dust from his clothes. Then, head down, clasping his hands behind his back, he walked off with his peculiar skating gait as if nothing had happened.

Dumbfounded, I stared after him until he turned off into a side street. Only then did I mount my bicycle and ride on. He certainly is odd, I thought.

My work was decided upon as soon as I arrived at

the organization section of the county Party committee. I was assigned temporarily to Flood Control Headquarters.

Its office was in a large house on the southern side of the compound. I was received by a young fellow about the same age as me.

"My name is Qin Yongchang. Just call me Old Qin . . . or Young Qin, if you like. It's up to you." Pointing around the room, he said, "This is our office. It's also our reception room and our dormitory. Maximum use of resources, you might say!"

Young Qin was a cheerful sort, and quite warm-hearted. As he talked, he helped me lay out my bedding and unpack my belongings. Then he brought me warm water to wash my face with and half a big watermelon. In less than an hour, we were old friends.

After a midday nap, Young Qin gave me a brief rundown on our work. Flood Control Headquarters was a temporary organization under the first secretary of the county Party committee. The actual day-to-day leadership was exercised by his second-in-command, Vice-director Tian of the Rural Construction Bureau.

"Come on," said Qin. "I'll introduce you."

The Rural Construction Bureau was diagonally across the road in a simple square compound of one-storey buildings. Tian's office was in the east wing. When we entered, he was seated writing at a desk.

Young Qin said, "The organization section has assigned us a new man, Old Tian."

"Good!" said Tian, without looking up.

"This is Comrade Peng Jie," Qin said hastily. "He's just graduated from the water conservancy school."

Only then did Tian put down his pen and raise his

head. I nearly jumped when I saw his face. What a coincidence! My "immediate superior" was the man I'd knocked down on the street that morning. Recalling my rudeness to him, I felt terribly embarrassed.

Like a gracious host, Qin brought forward a chair and poured me a drink of hot water from the thermos flask, then arranged the books and newspapers that were strewn over the desk into neat piles.

Old Tian didn't move. My first job, he said, was to familiarize myself with all the rivers and streams in the county; after that, there were several key villages he wanted me to visit. He spoke in a low voice, very slowly, as if he hadn't had a decent meal in a long time. When he finished telling me about my work, he suddenly said:

"You look kind of familiar. Haven't we met before? Ah, that's right. We've met."

"Where?" inquired Qin curiously.

Absolutely speechless, I went bright red. Luckily, someone came in just then with a document for Tian and I was saved any further embarrassment.

As we were returning to the flood control office, Qin pressed me to tell him how I had met Tian. I had no choice but to relate what had happened that morning.

"It's all right," Qin assured me. "He won't hold it against you. Don't worry about it."

"I was a little sore at the time," I said. "I kept ringing my bell, but he didn't even look up."

He laughed. "What good's a bell? An easy-going fellow like him — he wouldn't hear you if you fired a cannon!"

During that first week I saw little of Old Tian. He came to our office only twice and Qin and I went to his

place once to report on our work. From these few con-
tacts I got the impression that he was a very lethargic
person indeed. His abstracted air when he walked, his
listless way of talking, his casual approach to problems
— nothing seemed to arouse him. It was just my luck
to get a wash-out like that for a superior. But whatever
duties he gave me I performed to the best of my ability.

My main task then was to familiarize myself with
the work. At the same time I helped Qin push flood
control preparations in various townships. I studied the
maps of the county's waterways and went through a lot
of reference material. The county had three rivers, all
flowing from the mountains in the west to the plain in
the east.

These so-called rivers in fact were mostly dry beds.
There had been a big flood in August of 1954, but the
years that followed were uneventful. I didn't see much
likelihood of anything happening this year. The season
for floods was just about over, and there wasn't any sign
of rain.

On the night of the ninth day after my arrival
however, we were hit by a cloud-burst.

The sky had been clear all day but, towards evening,
clouds began to pile up in the west. It was about 10
p.m. and Young Qin had already climbed into bed.
I was sitting beside the table lamp reading aloud to
him from a novel when the telephone rang. The Water
Commission of Zhang Family Gully reported that mountain torrents were pouring into the Yongan River and
they estimated that its flow exceeded 100 cubic metres
per second.

I was shocked. According to the reports I'd read, the
Yongan hadn't moved that fast even in 1954. I hung up

and told Qin. Just as each of us seized separate phones and started to notify the villages lower down the river, a call came in from Anle Village. Their report nearly scared the life out of me. I threw down the phone and shouted:

"Anle has a breach in the dike!"

I dashed out of the room and ran to inform Tian. I got to his office in practically one breath, pushed open the door and plunged in. He had already gone to bed although his lamp was still lit.

"Get up, Old Tian!" I shouted. "The Yongan River is flooding! There's a breach in the dike at Anle!"

He propped himself up and asked, "Where in Anle is the breach?"

I told him it was east of the highway and already over forty feet wide. I thought he would jump right out of bed and hurry with me to headquarters. Still lying in bed, he said in a matter-of-fact way, "It's not that important. Some of the villages downstream will get a little less water for irrigation, that's all."

"Didn't you hear me?" I demanded angrily. "Anle has a break in the dike!"

"So what?" he said. "Anyhow, we can't stop it. Just let it flow."

I wanted to haul him out of bed and belt him one. How did he ever get to be leader of Flood Control Headquarters? I'd never met anyone so spineless!

Just then, Qin flew in through the door, crying, "Sancha River is rising too!"

Tian sat up, electrified. "What's the flow?" he asked urgently.

Qin said the secretary of Sancha Township had phoned. He hadn't been too sure of the rate of flow, but had said that the water was up to the rear of the Dragon King Temple.

"That means at least ninety cubic metres per second," said Old Tian. Throwing on his clothes, he instructed us: "Notify Haimen and Tianjia Villages to get everyone out on the dike, fast!"

Qin and I turned and ran.

By the time I reached the office, several people had arrived: Comrade Hao, the new secretary of the county Party committee; Comrade Wang, head of the committee's general office; Director Niu of the Military Service Bureau; and a number of cadres of the Rural Work Department. Obviously, Young Qin had let them know.

Some were phoning. Others were discussing the situation around a map of the county's watercourses. Everyone looked grim and the atmosphere in the room was tense. When they saw the two of us enter they asked anxiously, "Where's Old Tian?"

"He's on his way," said Qin.

I hurriedly put through a call to the village of Haimen. By the time I finished, Tian had already arrived, a walking-stick in one hand, his raincoat in the other. Although he was dressed the same as before his appearance had completely changed. He was full of energy, serious but cool. Striding into the room, he threw his things on to the bed, then walked over to the director of the Military Service Bureau.

"Round up all the standing militia and lead them to the south dike. You take charge personally!"

"Yes, sir!" Director Niu replied smartly, like a soldier acknowledging an order from his general. He turned on his heel and left.

To Comrade Wang, head of the county Party committee's general office, Old Tian said, "Get a car and have it waiting at the door." Then he picked up the telephone and began calling the different villages.

Everyone watched him silently. He shouted into the receiver: "Central, get me Du Village, Shangshe and Gucheng. . . . Du Village? Who's speaking? . . . This is Old Tian. Listen, open one sluice-gate of the third branch ditch. . . . What? You've opened all three of them already? I was afraid of that. You'd better close two right away. We built that sluice channel only last winter. It can't take that much water all at once. Stand by your dam. There's another big crest coming after midnight!"

Tian put down the phone and picked up another. He gave detailed instructions to Shangshe and Gucheng . . . what section of which dike should be watched, which channel gate should be opened, which should be closed, which emergency reservoir should be filled first, which second. . . . I quickly got the map of the county's water network and placed it on the table in front of him, but he didn't even glance at it. He seemed to know every ditch and its branches in the irrigation system.

Finishing his calls, Tian wiped the sweat off his brow. To the head of the general office he said, "Old Wang, you and Young Qin stay here and handle the phones. Secretary Hao, you and the others go back to bed. He turned to me. "You and I are going to Haimen. I'm afraid their south dike is in for trouble."

"The south dike is strong," I said. "It's their north dike that isn't so good." I had been to Haimen only the day before. This was one point I felt sure of.

"The gale's from the northeast," said Old Tian.

I had never noticed the wind direction.

"Your health is poor," Comrade Wang said to Old Tian. "Let me go. You look after things here."

"You couldn't manage," retorted Old Tian. He took his staff and raincoat and went out. I grabbed a padded jacket and followed.

A jeep was standing at the door for us. Old Tian said to the driver:

"Haimen. Step on it."

I hadn't dreamed Tian could be so authoritative and confident. But why had he been so unconcerned about the breach in the dike at Anle, and so upset over the rate of flow of the Sancha River? It was only 90 cubic metres per second. I knew that the Sancha used to cause lots of trouble, but in the past five years many flood control projects had been built along it. Only the previous winter several emergency reservoirs were constructed to take its overflow. Its lower reaches were very broad, and were capable of carrying a flow of up to 200 cubic metres per second. Surely 90 wasn't anything to get excited about.... Also, Tian had said there'd be another crest after midnight. How did he know?

In the car, I told him what was on my mind.

"Yongan River has a steep gradient, and its basin is small," Old Tian explained. "Its waters move fast, but in four hours at most the river is dry again. Could you plug the breach in four hours? Besides, a break there can't do much damage. All the fields east of the highway have long-stemmed crops. The water won't swamp them. From there the fields drain into the Bumper Harvest Canal, which leads north of the village to fields that seldom get enough water."

"What makes you say the Sancha River will have a flood crest after midnight?"

"No doubt about it. That 90 flow is just the water from the central branch. The mountain basins of the northern and southern branches have better retention; the water from those slopes won't come down till at least three hours later. That's after midnight, isn't it?"

Tian paused, then continued, "The Sancha gradient starts levelling out after it leaves the mountains. When it reaches the sand flats in Haimen gorge it's nearly flat. All that water piling up, and no place to drain off. It could be disastrous!"

Worried about Haimen, he lapsed into silence. I didn't say anything either. I remembered Qin telling me that Tian was the county's "home-made" flood conservancy expert. At the time I thought he was kidding but now I realized it was no joke. Listening to his analysis of the situation, I could tell he knew what he was talking about.

Haimen was about eleven kilometres from the county seat. A mile from Haimen, Old Tian told the driver to stop the jeep. "There's water in the second branch by now," he said. "You go on back." He got out and started walking. I followed.

It was a dark night with few stars and a northeast wind was blowing against us. Holding his walking-stick, Tian led the way. I tailed behind. He was moving so fast I almost had to run to keep up. When we reached the river-bed of the second branch, sure enough there was water in it. We waded across, but instead of entering the village of Haimen we followed a path leading directly to the southern dike.

Emerging from a field of tall sorghum, we could see

lanterns moving on the dike in the distance and we could hear faint shouts and the roar of water. Tian quickened his pace. I trotted panting behind him. When we climbed the dike, we found that the water was only one or two metres from the top. The dike was piled with straw mats, logs, sandbags.... People were bringing in materials, carrying earth to make the dike higher, endless lines coming and going, calling, shouting.

We cut our way through and travelled east along the dike until we reached the command post — a little shack surrounded by heaps of flood-fighting material. The small room was jammed. Secretary Zhai of the township Party committee, the Party secretaries of the villages of Haimen and Tianjia, the chairmen of the local people's communes had all turned up. Everyone looked glum. Tobacco smoke hung so thick you could hardly breathe.

"Hey, Old Tian!" someone cried joyfully as we entered the room.

Startled, everyone stood up. They all started speaking at once:

"Is that you, Old Tian?"

"I knew you'd come!"

"You're here at last!"

The men's expression brightened. Their voices were full of emotion. Obviously, everyone had great confidence in Tian. It was as if now that he had arrived they weren't afraid of the flood waters no matter how big they might grow.

Tian asked what material had been prepared, how many men had been organized for an emergency squad, how fast the river was rising.

"The bed was only half filled an hour ago. You've seen where it is now," the township Party secretary responded.

Tian thought a moment. "The water from the north branch is starting to come down. It'll get worse before long. Set those mat breakwaters up along the dike in a hurry. The wind's not showing any signs of dying."

Several men ran out to execute his orders.

Old Tian's eyes swept the room. "Why isn't Old Man Jiang here?" he asked.

"It didn't seem that serious," Jin, the Haimen Party secretary, responded. "So we didn't call him."

"We can't afford to take any chances," Tian snapped, reaching for the telephone. Jin said the line was broken. Somebody was out repairing it now. Pushing the phone aside, Tian said, "Go back to the village and ask him to come." Turning his head, he said to me, "You go with him. Phone Director Niu from the village and tell him to put mat breakwaters up on the dike at the county seat right away. Tell him to pay special attention to the section at Wangjia Slope."

Everyone was busy putting up mat breakwaters as we walked along the dike. I overheard a couple of men talking.

"Now that Old Tian's here, we don't have to worry," said one.

"Not worry?" retorted the other. "If there wasn't any danger he wouldn't have come!"

"It can't be too bad," said the first man. "Old Man Jiang still hasn't shown up!"

In a low voice I asked Jin about Old Man Jiang.

"Breach repair expert," said Jin. "Sending for him means we're really in for trouble." He sighed. "If this dike really goes, seven villages south of here will be under water!"

I felt very depressed. If this were next year, there'd be no problem. In the autumn a big reservoir was going to be built on the river's upper reaches. I had seen the plan in the county office.

We hurried down the channel and soon reached Haimen Village. While I made my phone call, Jin went for Jiang and before long returned, supporting a white-bearded old man. He appeared to be at least seventy and was so shaky when he walked, I was afraid he was going to fall. But he still refused to let Jin get him a donkey.

"You go on first," he said. "I'll get there a little later. If there's trouble, it won't be till after midnight anyway."

"Go ahead, Old Jin," I urged. "I'll look after old uncle."

Jin hurried off towards the dike. The old man and I slowly followed, with me supporting him on my arm.

"How's Old Tian's ailment?" the old man asked me. "Better?"

"What ailment?" I countered.

"You mean you don't know? His legs were so bad last winter, he couldn't get out of bed. He's got what-do-you-call-it? Ah, that's right — rheumatism!"

No wonder Tian always moved so slowly and wore padded trousers even in the hottest weather. I suddenly remembered how quickly he'd walked when we got out of the jeep. It must have been awfully painful!

Old Man Jiang liked to talk. "Old Tian got his rheumatism in 1954. We'd had a lot of rain that autumn. The whole region was flooded. Old Tian was out in that weather, wading from village to village, for seven days and seven nights, leading the flood fighting. By the time the water receded, both his legs were badly swollen." The old man heaved a sigh. "He certainly gets things done! Even better than his father did!" He went on to tell me about Tian's background.

Tian came from Tianjia Village, a kilometre away from Haimen. His father had been good friends with Jiang, and was a famous swimmer. Whenever there was a breach in the dike, these two, and a few others, took charge of repairs. There was a commission set up by the county government in those days to control the river, but its officials were only interested in embezzling the large sums of money contributed by the local people for harnessing the river and the dike was always in disrepair. It crumbled at least twice a year whenever there was even a hint of flooding. When that happened the officials invariably disappeared. They certainly never showed their faces on the dike.

In his early teens, Tian was already helping his father and Jiang with dike work. The boy was courageous, thorough and energetic. By the age of twenty he'd built up a considerable reputation in the region.

After Liberation, the county government appointed him as a water conservancy technician. Tian was everywhere — deepening the rivers, digging irrigation canals. . . . Later he took courses for several months in a special school run by the regional government. Many of the water control projects in the county had been designed by him.

We had already reached the southern dike. Old Man Jiang didn't want to go up it, but insisted that we walk along through the fields in the rear and only mount the dike at the command post. When I asked him why he laughed.

"If people see me, they'll think it's a bad sign."

When we arrived at the command post the room was quiet. Only Tian and a young woman doctor were there. Tian was saying to her, "You stay here and take phone calls. Don't leave even if the sky collapses!"

Evidently the phone had been repaired. When Tian caught sight of us, he rushed up to shake hands warmly.

"How does it look?" the old man asked him. "Is the dike going to last the night?"

Tian frowned. "The wind's too strong. It's dangerous. Uncle, rest here on the brick bed. We'll call you when we need you. I'm going to take a look at the east end."

I followed him out.

The water was much more turbid than when I had left for the village. Although it was still a metre from the top of the dike, the wind whipped it into huge waves flinging up the froth. Were it not for the mat breakwaters, the dike would never have been able to bear up under the pounding. Tian and I hadn't gone very far before our shoes and socks were soaked by flying spray.

Suddenly there was a tremendous crash, followed by the urgent beating of a big gong. The alarm signal. That could mean only one thing — a section of the dike had collapsed.

Without waiting for Tian's order I turned and raced to the command headquarters to get Jiang. The emergency squad was running towards the break, carrying supplies and pressure lamps. At the door of the command post I met Jiang coming out.

"Where is it?" he shouted. "Where is it?"

I pointed east. He started off and I hurried to help him, but he pushed my arm aside and strode off. I was baffled. How had his old legs suddenly become so agile?

At the danger spot, the lamps were burning brightly. People shouted and ran back and forth, delivering sandbags. When they saw Jiang, the crowd quickly divided to let him through. We reached the break. It was over seven metres wide and tumbling muddy water was roaring through it.

Tian was directing the placing of sandbags. He had his back to us but from his gestures and the tone of his voice it was plain that he wasn't frightened in the least. On the contrary, he seemed cooler and steadier than before.

The sandbags were useless and were swept away by surging water. The breach was growing wider as the edges of the break continued to crumble. Secretary Zhai and Old Jin and their men on the other side were also trying to fill in sandbags but their efforts were in vain.

Jiang silently inspected the scene. Finally, he shouted, "Stop!"

Tian turned around and saw the old man. "What now? Shall we drive in stakes?"

"Yes, but we've got to strengthen the ends of the break first."

"You give the orders!" said Tian. Turning to me, he said, "Telephone the county to warn them. . . . But tell them we definitely will plug the breach! Definitely!" His voice was firm, confident.

Weaving my way through the noisy crowd, I hurried back to the small shack.

By the time I had made my call and returned, things were much more orderly. People were lined up in two rows on top of the dike. They were steadily passing along stakes, mats, sandbags. . . . I walked around them to the edge of the break. Five stakes had already been planted, starting at the edge and advancing towards the middle, with sandbags piled in front of them. This section was already up to the water level. Jiang stood by chanting cadence for the men driving in the sixth stake. Tian and some others continued to pile sandbags.

On the opposite side of the break, Secretary Zhai was supervising men driving another row of stakes in our direction. The hammering of the stakes, the chanted cadence, the roar of the water, the howling of the wind . . . created a tense, ominous atmosphere.

The work proceeded smoothly. Slowly the gap narrowed. Some time after three in the morning, a breach of only four metres or so remained. It looked as if we'd close it soon but then a powerful rush of water swept away the stakes half driven in, taking Jiang and several young pile-drivers with them. Their safety ropes kept them from being washed very far and a dozen helping hands hauled them back to the dike.

Jiang was dripping wet. His face was ashen and he trembled violently. "We can't plug this one!" he panted to Tian, as he crawled to his feet. "It's too much for me!"

Hearing this, the men standing around were quite alarmed.

"Let the people go home while there's still time," the old man pleaded. "They ought to start working on the village dikes. Otherwise the villages will be finished too!"

His listeners became even more panicky. There were excited discussions. Several men turned to run.

"Don't move, any of you!" glowered Old Tian. His eyes were fierce.

Everyone froze and for a moment there was absolute silence. Old Tian turned on Old Man Jiang like a tiger.

"That breach must be filled!"

To the other side of the break, he shouted: "Old Zhai, organize your men immediately. We're going into the water!"

At once, we could hear Secretary Zhai calling through his megaphone, "All Party members and Youth Leaguers who know how to swim, step forward. Get ready to go in!"

While shouting to the men in the rear to hurry with sandbags and stakes, Tian was removing his notebook and fountain pen from his pocket. He was obviously going in too.

"Old Tian, you can't," I urged him. "You've got rheumatism!"

He glared at me and thrust his belongings into my hands. Turning to the crowd, he yelled: "Those who can swim, come with me!"

There was a hasty exchange among the men.

"Old Tian's going in!"

"What are we waiting for?"

Five or six young fellows ran up, then more, and more.... Arm in arm, they formed a long chain. Tian jumped in first. The water was up to their waists, then up to their chests. The raging river knocked them staggering, but they continued to drive across. A human chain led by Secretary Zhai struggled towards them from the opposite side. Three times Zhai and Tian almost touched hands, but each time huge waves smashed them apart.

Squatting on the dike, Jiang rose abruptly to his feet. To the men around him, he cried, "Bring a long telephone pole, quick!" When the pole was brought, he instructed them to throw it across the breach, then he called to the men in the water, "Grab it! Grab the pole!"

Tian and Secretary Hao dragged themselves along it until they could clasp hands. A solid human chain was formed from one end of the break to the other, with the people leaning against the pole. At this, other men, shouting, jumped into the water hand in hand to make a second and third row directly behind them. The river could never break this barrier.

Wave after wave broke on the heads of the human barricade. When a wave struck, the men vanished. Only when it receded did they appear — choking on the muddy water, gasping for breath, getting ready for the next wave. . . .

We on the dike were also very busy. Jiang counted cadence and directed the men driving the stakes. I and others were rapidly piling sandbags into the breach that were passed to us by the rows of people along the dike. The wind and waves pushed in relentlessly, but the men in the water stood firm.

An hour passed. The line of driven stakes stretched across the breach, forming the backing for growing piles of sandbags. Gradually, the break narrowed as the sandbags mounted higher and higher. . . .

It was darker now and much colder. Though I was standing on the dry dike dressed in a padded jacket,

I was still shivering. I could see the men in the icy water clenching their teeth against the wind and the waves and the cold. Tian stood like a rock. He kept shouting:

"Hold on! Hold on and we'll win!"

He seemed to be exhorting not only the others but also himself as well.

By dawn the breach was closed at last and the flood waters were locked in the river-bed. When Jiang cried, "She's closed!" everyone cheered. Shouting for joy, men crawled out of the water on to the dike. They were trembling with cold and plastered with mud from head to foot, but on each man's face was a happy grin. They crowded around bonfires which had been prepared in advance, and dried out.

Only Tian remained in the water, his eyes closed, his teeth clenched. Hands clutching the telephone pole, he lay motionless on top of a sandbag.

Frightened, I yelled, "Save him! Save Old Tian!"

Secretary Zhai, Jiang and a few others hurried over and dragged him on to the dike. He was unconscious. Both legs were drawn up in a tight cramp and his breath was very faint.

We rushed him to the command post shack. Secretary Zhai ordered some men to prepare a stretcher, then called the county and told them to send a car immediately. We removed Tian's soaking garments. Jiang, tears in his eyes, took off his own gown and gently covered Tian with it. I stripped off my padded jacket and laid it on Tian's legs. From outside the shack, men passed in their own dry clothes. People crowded the doorway, anxiously wanting to know how Old Tian was.

The young woman doctor quickly gave him two injections and rubbed his legs with turpentine. His knees were red and swollen and the veins in his calves stood out in bumpy knots.

The stretcher was ready. Someone had run into the village and brought back two thick quilts. When we laid Tian on the stretcher everyone wanted to carry it. As we left the shack and came out on the dike, the sun had already risen from behind the mountains and the wind had died. The river was flowing quietly. The men on the dike gazed at the stretcher, very moved. When we crossed the second branch, a car was waiting. We placed Tian in it and went directly to the county hospital.

Two months later, Old Tian was out. Once again it was on the street that I saw him. He was still the same — shoulders hunched, head down, hands behind his back, his walk slow and stately.

Watching him approach, I was greatly moved. He didn't seem at all odd now. He was my first superior on my first job, an unassuming, hard-working man rightly respected by everyone.

April 1959

Translated by Yin Yishi

Ma Feng was born in Xiaoyi County, Shanxi Province in 1922. He joined the Eighth Route Army at 16 and in 1940 attended the Lu Xun Institute of Literature and Art at Yan'an. He subsequently worked as a journalist and editor. He col-

laboraied *with another writer,* Xi Rong, *on the novel* Heroes of the Lüliang Mountains *and then produced* A Biography of Liu Hulan, *the film script* The Young People of Our Village, *a collection of short stories* Village Hatred. My First Superior *exemplifies his concise, fluent style.*

He is now vice-chairman of the Shanxi Federation of Literary and Art Circles.

Dajee and Her Father

Gao Ying

IT has been several months since I left Liangshan Mountains, the home of the Yi people who had lived in slavery until Liberation ten years before. Every evening after work when my little daughter threw herself into my arms, put her soft little hands round my neck and nestled her warm face against mine, I let myself relax in the joys of being a father. It was at such moments that the face of a young girl from Liangshan and that of her father would come before my eyes. I want to tell you their story, a tale of love and hate. That is why I've brought out my diary and copied the following pages.

June 7   Fair

After a whole day's ride on horseback and asking my way numerous times, I at last arrived in the little village of Jiagu. At the edge of the village, I met the co-operative chairman Shama Muya, an old acquaintance of mine from the people's congress of the autonomous *zhou*. He greeted me warmly, took the reins of my horse and walked into the village by my side.

Shama is a middle-aged man with an open, cheerful and rugged face. Only the deep lines on his forehead reveal his bitter past. We sat opposite each other across the hearth as he told me about co-op affairs, a pipe between his teeth. He mentioned the name of Maherha, a member of the co-operative managing committee, who seemed to be sulking lately. Maherha showed little interest in his work and even failed to appear at co-op meetings. Poor Shama's face darkened, as if all the black clouds in the sky had cast their dark shadows on it.

"He's dissatisfied with the co-op's farming then?" I asked.

"Never heard him complain in that respect."

"Are you people good to him?" I tried again.

"Why not?" he replied without hesitation. "We are all 'sons of the hearth'* who suffered plenty. Our hearts are bound close together."

I was puzzled. I had to get to the bottom of this. "How old is Maherha?"

"How old? . . . Ah, he doesn't even know that himself. Probably past sixty."

"Has he got a family?"

"He has a daughter in her late teens; her name's Dajee. . . ." he answered slowly passing his pipe to me.

"Do they have a hard time still?"

"How can that be? He is emancipated now. He has built himself a new house and gets enough to eat and warm clothes to wear. Only the other day he bought a new pleated skirt for Dajee."

---

* Slaves.

I asked no more but sat silently smoking.

June 8   Fair

Before supper, Shama took me to visit Maherha. Thick, greyish, white smoke oozed out of a narrow door. Supper was cooking.

"Maherha!" Shama called.

"Come in," a heavy voice trailed out with the smoke.

My eyes watered as I entered the door. When I recovered slightly, I noticed a man by the hearth, his head covered by a black kerchief and a dark grey wool cape over his shoulders.

"Maherha, Comrade Li has come to see you," said Shama.

I was sure he would offer me a seat with a friendly gesture, that was the least he could do under the circumstances. But he didn't even say hello. I sat down silently opposite him as he continued with bowed head to poke at the damp faggots in the hearth.

"Where's Dajee?" asked Shama.

"Still digging the fields," Maherha answered in a low, husky voice.

"What are you cooking for your daughter?" I asked, eager to join in the talk.

"Vegetable soup," he smiled wryly.

I seized the opportunity to continue, "It's smoking hard. You should pile the faggots up a little."

He made no reply, but continued to sit there coldly.

The fire got going and the smoke gradually dispersed. Shama and the old man began discussing the building of an irrigation ditch. As I listened with half an ear I observed Maherha closely. He seemed very old. His thin, dark, sallow face, coarse as tree bark, was heavily lined. A few deep furrows cut across his prominent forehead like imprints of a heavy whip. His small brown eyes squinted in the firelight as, back bent, he stretched hands bony as dry pine twigs towards the fire. The sight of this old man brought the dark shadow of slavery to my eyes: heavy leather whip whistling over bare backs, iron fetters clanking, hard labour, wild herbs and disease. My heart was heavy.

"Grandad Maherha, do you do the cooking for your daughter every day?" I asked.

He nodded.

"What a good father you are," I said loudly.

"Maherha is a very fond father," Shama put in. "Every time he gets his share of income from the co-op he hastens to the county town to get beads or some pretty cotton cloth for Dajee." At the mention of his daughter, a faint smile floated to Maherha's lips, but it vanished just as quickly.

"Comrade Li," he blurted out suddenly, "are there bad men still among you Han people?" His small narrow eyes, enmeshed in a network of wrinkles, were pinned on me. I was taken aback. It was the first time such a question was addressed to me in Liangshan.

"There are some bad men still," I answered, "such as bad landlords and rich peasants who refuse to abide by the law; there are some petty thieves too...."

Just then we heard a cackling and flapping of wings outside and the voice of a young girl calling to the chickens. Then one hand holding up her long skirt, a girl of about seventeen entered the door.

Maherha's head turned to her at once. "Come and have your supper, Dajee," he said, his husky voice full of warmth.

The girl sat down close to him. *"Abda,** our chickens are always straying into the fields to peck at the vegetables."* Her voice was sweet as spring water gurgling in the valley. Glancing at me out of bright black eyes, she cocked her head a little to ask, "Where did you come from?"

"From the other side of heaven," I answered teasingly.

"But I can see you haven't got wings," she laughed merrily.

Her hair, plaited into a thick black braid and adorned with little red beads, was coiled on top of her head over which was draped a small black kerchief with embroidered edgings. A tight black cotton blouse hugged her young breasts. There was a strand of pretty red pearls round her neck. Her skirt, spread out on the ground, seemed a round lotus leaf floating on water. Her face was round and smooth; her features small and even. I was surprised that she had not the heavy contours and sharp lines of the Yi girls. Instead, her eyes were soft and two tiny dimples danced in her cheeks. Really, she did not resemble her father in the least.

Dajee began to ask me about construction in the Han areas. When I told her about factories, airplanes, trolley-buses ... she listened wide-eyed, her eyebrows delicately arched.

To my surprise, old Maherha cut me short coldly. "Dajee, our Liangshan government will see to all that too in the future. Eat your supper now."

As he handed me a ball of cooked buckwheat, he asked me another strange question. "You said there are

---

* Father.

still bad men among the Hans. Would they be coming here to bully us and kidnap our people again?"

Before I had a chance to answer, Dajee said, "Don't talk nonsense, *Ahda*. Who dares to bully us now?"

Maherha sank into a silence from which he did not rouse even when we took our leave.

June 11   Fair

Time to plant the maize. Our Yi brethren all went to work in the fields. Black capes and coloured skirts bedecked the hillside.

Dajee and I worked together. I dug holes and she put seeds into them. A little bamboo basket on her left arm, she sowed deftly and accurately, her bare feet stepping across the soft soil.

"Dajee, why is it you Yi people will not use animal manure?" I asked.

"The Yis, they're superstitious, that's why," she replied.

The hoe in my hands shook. "Aren't you superstitious then?" I asked. "And why do you say 'they'?"

She only smiled, refusing to answer. After a while as we continued working, she said, "Comrade Li, don't you think I look like a Han?" I put down my hoe to scrutinize her face closely.

"So . . . you are a Han?" I was surprised.

She gave me a wink and smiled. "Hurry up and dig, or we'll fall behind."

When I returned from the fields my first words to Shama were, "So Dajee is a Han!"

He smiled, revealing even, white teeth. "A person with good eyesight spots a green larch the moment he raises his head," he said.

"When did she come to Liangshan?" I pursued.

"It happened more than ten years ago," he said slowly, chewing his pipe. "Ahou, the slave-owner, kidnapped her from the villages in the foothills. Dajee was not much taller than the stove then."

"Then what is Maherha to her?"

"Maherha is her *Ahda*." He went on to explain, "Old Maherha used to be one of Ahou's slaves too. The slave-owner tormented and beat the little girl so cruelly that old Maherha took to protecting her; he loved her and treated her like a daughter. Dajee began calling him *Ahda*, though in front of the master, she dared not. For fifty years, Maherha had suffered as a slave. It was not until after the democratic reform that he built himself a home and made Dajee his daughter...."

Shama's tone was sad as he went over the poor old man's life. Maherha's face, rough as tree bark, and his hands, bony as dry twigs — imprints of slavery — floated to my mind. I sensed vaguely that old Maherha's brooding and his coolness towards me had something to do with his daughter, Dajee.

"Are they fond of each other, Dajee and her father?" I asked Shama.

"Oh, very, they are as inseparable as the squirrel and the pine tree."

Suddenly I remembered the queer questions Maherha addressed to me the other day. "Then why is Maherha unhappy and sulking?" I asked, some inkling of the answer dawning on me. "Maybe some Han has been bullying him?"

"Only the forest knows the thoughts in the song-bird's head," Shama's answer was like a riddle.

June 12 Overcast

I have to find Dajee and get to the bottom of this. This morning, I saw her go to the stream for water and went after her.

"Dajee, I want to ask you something. You. . . ."

She sat down on a flat boulder. Her eyes, warm and trusting, were fixed on me as she said, "I am a Han. But I don't know where I was born or who my parents are. My earliest memory is the cruel wolf-like face of the slave-owner. . . . He beat me and burned me with branches, red hot from the hearth, all because I hadn't the strength to push a big millstone taller than my head. Look, Comrade Li. . . ."

She rolled up her sleeve and showed me the scars on her arm. My eyes faltered at the sight. I couldn't bear to look. She stared into the distance as she went on, like one talking in her sleep:

"The master made me go up the hill for dry wood in the deep snow. If I didn't get enough, he gave me no food. This went on day after day. I ate only wild herbs from the hills and munched snow. When I was worn out from hunger, it was Maherha who slipped me bits of buckwheat dough."

She was weeping, big tears trickling down her face. "Once a leopard got one of the master's sheep and he cursed me for being a useless shepherd. He tied me to a tree in the woods with leather thongs and said I deserved to be eaten by the wild beasts. Though Maherha pleaded with him to spare me, he would not relent. It was a terrifying night. The wind roared through the woods and I closed my eyes, waiting for death. Then Maherha came stealthily, untied the thongs and carried me back. The wicked master got so angry he beat him until poor Maherha passed out. . . ."

Tears filled my eyes. I wiped them furtively with my sleeve.

"I wanted to escape, but where could I go? Where was there a home for me? I didn't know of any place without leopards and slave-owners. I cried for my father and mother, but no one came to comfort me or stroke my hair. There was only Maherha who in the icy cold night hugged me tightly to warm me and who covered me with his ragged wool cape."

Dajee's sad past made my blood boil. I wanted to say to her, "My poor little sister, I'll take you away from Liangshan tomorrow, take you back to the Han people. I'll help you find your father and mother. . . ."

Very quickly though, reason had the better of my emotions. Instead of bursting out, I said soothingly, "Don't cry any more, little Dajee. The slave-owners have been overthrown and the people of Liangshan have risen to their feet. They are now as free and happy as the Hans. It's the same now everywhere in China. . . ."

Dajee looked at me with wet eyes. "Yes, I know. It's good everywhere in China now, that's why I don't want to leave Liangshan and my *Ahda* Maherha. Comrade Li, you must investigate this matter carefully, and see whether that man is really. . . ."

Her sudden reference to some man confused me. "Dajee, what are you talking about?"

"Haven't you come to our village to help that man find out about me?"

"Which man?"

"That old man of Han nationality."

"I don't understand you, Dajee. I've come here to help look after farming in the co-op."

"My *Ahda* said you came here to find out about me and told me not to speak to you."

At my confusion, Dajee smiled with tears in her eyes. Taking a long breath, she started from the very beginning.

"Last month I went to the county town to sell vegetables. An old Han kept staring at me. When I sat under the city gate, he sat near me. Later, I rested for a while on the curb and he went and sat down opposite me. Finally he came over to ask my name. I heard him mutter to himself, 'She looks just like my daughter ... there's a pink birthmark on her face too. ... '"

I peered at Dajee. Sure enough, there was a small pink mark on her right cheek.

"I got a little frightened," Dajee continued. "So I walked away with my vegetable basket. The old man came after me and asked, 'Where do you live, child?' There were tears in his old eyes. I took pity on him and told him the name of our village. I could feel his eyes on my back as I walked away.

"I heard him mutter, 'I must get the county government's help ... I'll go to the county government. ...' Comrade Li, don't you think there was something wrong with that old man's head?"

For a few seconds I was silent, overwhelmed by the complex situation Dajee had just described. Then things became clear. I understood why Maherha was worried, why he treated me so coolly and why he asked the strange questions about bad men.

"Don't think too much of the incident," I tried to

soothe Dajee. "Maybe he mistook you for someone else."

"Yes, he might have been mistaken." She breathed a light sigh.

June 19   Rain

The tragic and joyful event which I dreaded and yet half-expected finally happened.

The sky was dark. A drizzle started from early morning. An old man, a Han, came to see me. He wore a big straw hat, homespun blue cotton suit and straw sandals plastered with mud. He was thin with sharp shoulder blades showing. Wrinkles covered his forehead and ran down to the corners of his eyes. A straggly grey beard adorned his chin. Removing his wet straw hat, with quivering hands he produced a letter of introduction from the county Party committee:

> This is to introduce Ren Pinqing, a poor peasant of Han nationality who wishes to look for his daughter Niuniu in your village. Please give him all possible assistance. If his daughter is not to be found, take care of him and send him home. If the daughter is in your village, he must show concrete proof to identify her. Don't make any final decision but refer the case back to the county Party committee for further directions.

I consulted the co-op chairman, Shama, and we decided to question the old man first.

"How do you know," I asked, "that this girl you saw is your daughter?"

The old man blinked as he stammered, "She is, she

definitely is my Niuniu. Niuniu was kidnapped by some Yi people when she was six and taken into Liangshan Mountains. . . . She was the exact image of her mother . . . brows, eyes, face. . . ."

"Do you have proof to show that she is your daughter?" asked Shama.

"I have, but I won't tell you. I'll say it in front of the child. . . ." His tone and his determination confirmed our impression that we had met with a very obstinate old man. We sent for Dajee.

She came into the room hesitantly, her hands behind her back. At the door she paused and stared at the old man with startled soft eyes. The old man regarded her sadly, lips trembling. Both were silent.

"I can't," Dajee suddenly burst out. "I can't go with him. What right has he to say I'm his daughter?"

Old Man Ren was stunned. He rubbed his knees nervously with rough thin hands. "I only . . . only . . . came to see," he faltered, hanging his head. "If she's not my daughter, all right . . . I. . . ."

"Please give us your proof now," Shama urged.

The old man wiped his eyes with the hem of his tunic and sighed. "Her name was Niuniu," he began slowly. "She had a round face, small mouth and two little dimples."

"What kind of proof is that!" said Shama.

The old man shot me a glance and continued, "She was called Niuniu and looked like her mother. That year, she was not quite six, her mother took ill and I went to the market for medicine. Niuniu was playing by herself on the meadow outside our door when suddenly two mounted Yi people came, wrapped her in a felt rug and took her away. They went towards Liangshan. . . ."

I listened, my eyes on Dajee. She stood where she was, face pale and eyes glazed.

"For more than a year, I searched everywhere in Liangshan and questioned the kind ones among the Yi people but nobody knew anything about such a little girl. A dozen years went by and I'd given up hope. I never expected to see her last month in the county town. She looks exactly like her mother and also there's a pink mark on her right cheek. . . ."

"Look here, old uncle," I protested mildly, "anybody can identify her that way. The pink mark is there for all to see."

The old man was silent for a few minutes, his eyes on Dajee. "She is the image of her mother. . . . Also there are tooth prints left by a dog bite on her left leg . . . four tooth prints a little above the left knee."

Dajee's left hand stole to the hem of her skirt, gripped it tightly and then loosened it. With a sharp cry she sat down on her heels and buried her face in her hands. Ren was at first startled and then, as if waking from a dream, stretched both hands out to her, "Niuniu, you are my Niuniu. . . ."

Dajee's tear-stained eyes appeared above her hands. Soft as a summer breeze, came her muffled "*Abda!*" The old man stumbled towards his daughter.

"Niuniu," he said with a sob. "Remember the two-room thatched hut we lived in? There were three pomegranate trees at the door. Remember?"

Dajee shook her head.

"Try to remember. Not far from our door there was

a pond. You used to shoo the ducklings home from the pond every evening."

Dajee leaned her head weakly against the wall and stared at the ceiling.

"Remember the bamboo fence by our gate, child, and how you used to count the number of sticks. . . ."

Dajee suddenly flung herself into Old Man Ren's arms; her shoulders quivering with suppressed sobs. Her father was also crying. . . .

My eyes were also moist, but before I had time to wipe them, an angry roar came from the door.

"Who dares come to take away my Dajee?" It was Maherha.

I stood up, my muscles tense. Dajee also flinched. Old Maherha rushed in like a whirlwind, his shirt open. Standing in the middle of the room, he fixed eyes, red with hate, on Old Man Ren.

"Get out of here," he cried fiercely. "Get out!"

I had heard about the strong temperament of the Liangshan people but I never expected such fury from old, emaciated Maherha. I was also surprised that thin, old Ren could retaliate with such heat.

"Shut up, you savage," he shouted back, his voice rumbling like thunder. "The girl is mine."

Maherha's face darkened, the wrinkles on his face tight as bow-strings, his brown eyes looking ready to burst from their sockets. "I'll kill you," he said, the words spewing out through grimly set teeth. With a sudden jerk, he pulled a rusted dagger from his belt.

Shama caught his hand in time.

"Maherha!" he admonished sternly.

Unable to free his hand, Maherha turned on me. "Didn't you tell me that the Hans will not bully us again? But this man is here to take my daughter from me! He calls me a savage. You fooled me!"

"He should not call you a savage," said Shama. "But look at your own behaviour. You want to kill him, kill a Han in the Yi area. You are bullying our Han brothers."

Maherha had no answer for that. He weakened. Turning to Dajee, he said in a soft quivering voice, "Dajee, my daughter, you cannot go with him, you are mine."

"That's right, *Abda*," said Dajee, tears in her eyes. "I cannot leave you. But for you, I would have been dead long ago."

Maherha stretched out one hand. "Let us go home then, Dajee, come." It was more of an entreaty than a command.

Dajee left with Maherha. As she went through the door, she gave a parting glance at the other old man.

Ren gripped my arm. "Comrade Li, the county Party committee sent me to you. I must ask you for my daughter."

"This matter involves the solidarity of our two fraternal peoples. That's why you can't take your daughter away with you today. Go home. You'll hear from us soon." I tried to reassure him.

"All right," he said after a long pause. "I'll wait. But I warn you, if you don't give me back my daughter I shall complain higher up: I'll even go to Chairman Mao."

Shama and I accompanied the old man a long way out of the village. We did all we could to reassure him.

June 20   Fair

I went to the county Party committee and told the Party secretary about Dajee and her fathers in detail. The secretary's instructions were clear: Dajee must decide which father she wants to live with. Her decision must be clearly explained to the two old men. We should make use of this occasion to strengthen the solidarity between the Yis and the Hans.

June 21   Overcast

Expecting a cold reception, I went to visit Maherha again. To my surprise, the old man stood up respectfully to offer me a seat and gave me some tobacco. Dajee nodded a silent greeting. Old Maherha came to the point at once.

"You are sent by the Party committee of the Liangshan autonomous *zhou* I believe you will not take sides and think only of the Han."

"You are right."

"That old man is Dajee's real father but Dajee has no love for him. She would rather stay with me always."

I glanced at Dajee.

She met my eyes and nodded. "Yes, I've made up my mind not to leave *Ahda*." This *Ahda* referred of course to Maherha.

The problem is simpler now. Since Dajee will not leave Maherha, all we need do is explain the matter to Old Man Ren and make him see reason.

June 23   Rain

The rain keeps falling maddeningly, making the hills and dales very muddy. I stayed at home today, reading alone by the hearth.

Dajee came in without a sound and sat down on her heels by my side. Her face was very pale. A lock of wet black hair was plastered to her white forehead; her big eyes were sad and sunken. There was no sign of the merry laughter that usually hovered round her lips. Her brows were tightly knit. She seemed to have matured overnight.

"Comrade Li," she said in a low voice.

"Has something happened, Dajee?" I asked.

She shook her head. "Will you help me write a letter?" she asked. When I wanted to know to whom, she said, "To my *Ahda*." My heart tightened as if caught by an invisible hand.

"All right Dajee, you dictate and I'll take it down for you." I spread a piece of paper on my book and she began.

Dear *Ahda*,

This is your Niuniu writing to you. I'm thinking of you; I'm sure you are longing for me too. . . . Will you come and see me again?

When you come you must take the big road. Avoid the forest paths for there are leopards there. Wear a pair of sturdy sandals when you come so that the pebbles will not cut your feet, and wear a cape so you won't get wet in the rain. When you get thirsty don't drink the cold water from the stream but go to the village and ask them for a bowl of warm water. . . .

My pen shook. This was no ordinary letter; every word revealed the love of a daughter for a long-lost father. Dajee, her long black lashes cast down, sat silent now. "Is that all?" I asked.

"That's all. . . ." Her lips hardly moved. Her voice was like the chill wind soughing through the forest leaves at night.

June 25   Overcast

I met Maherha at the edge of the maize field. His eyes were not only cold but they gleamed icily like the sharp edges of a knife. Stretching out bony hands, he blocked my way.

"Hanua,"* he called fiercely.

I halted.

"What have you been telling Dajee?" he demanded in a menacing voice. "I know you want to take her away from me. You were sent by the Party committee of our autonomous *zhou* but you are not working for us Yi people. You think only of the Hans. If you succeed in sending Dajee away, don't think I'll let you remain. I'll drive you. . . ."

"What reason have you to accuse me like that, Grandad Maherha?" I asked quietly. "If you could weigh my heart on a scale, you would find that it balances fairly between you and the other old man. My heart acts only according to the orders of our government."

Maherha seized my hand. "Please help me, Comrade Li," he pleaded in a hoarse voice. "Please save my Dajee. She has not eaten properly for two days. . . .

---

* A rude name for Han.

She is changed and is wasting away. Her heart is sick. At night she wakes up sobbing and crying for her *Abda.* ... Save us and I'll be grateful always. As long as it's for her good, I'll even let her go away, I mean it. ..."

I was too listless to do anything when I got home.

Shama sat opposite me by the hearth poking at the fire. Blue smoke coiled round us.

"I used to believe in demons and imagined that all the sufferings of humanity were manufactured by them," he said. "Now I know there are no demons. But some of the pains and agony made by that real demon, slavery, has not yet been completely wiped out in Liangshan."

June 29   Fair

Shama and I decided to call an emergency meeting of the co-op committee. Old Man Ren came again, declaring firmly that this time he would take his daughter away.

The meeting was held outdoors under the sun. It turned into more of a village than a co-op meeting because almost all the villagers turned up. Everyone was concerned about Dajee. From the way people were seated, I had an idea of their feelings. A dozen or so villagers sat scattered here and there these were taking no sides but meant to leave everything to the co-op committee. A group of young girls sat with Dajee; a plump one held her hand protectively. Three old men sat by Maherha, each with a white stone pipe between his lips. I could hear one mutter. "Just refuse, Maherha. No one can snatch Dajee away. ..." Only the young book-keeper Erhbu sat by Old Man Ren; he had volunteered to be Ren's interpreter.

Both Maherha and Ren looked awful. Their faces were pale and haggard. Now and then their eyes met and they exchanged glances, neither of hate nor of friendliness, but a kind of helpless despair. Maherha eyed the little cloth bundle in Ren's hands with suspicion.

Shama addressed the meeting. At first he spoke formally about unity between the different nationalities of our country, then he warmed up and talked with real feelings. . . .

". . . The Hans and the Yis were brothers in ancient times. In those days there were no quarrels or fights. The Hans gave the Yis grain in return for which they got oxen and sheep. Later, magistrates appeared among the Hans and slave-owners among the Yis. They fought and wanted to break one another's backs. These magistrates and slave-owners sucked the blood of the Han peasants and the Yi slaves and made them live in tears. . . ."

Everyone was silent. An eagle flew past overhead. . . .

"The chickens do nothing to annoy the eagle but it comes to seize the chicks. When the chicks are taken away, the mother hen cackles in sorrow. Dajee was a Han; she was kidnapped and brought to Liangshan by the slave-owner. Maherha had a hard life and no home of his own. He loves Dajee though she is not his real daughter. Who is it who brewed this bitter wine?"

People's heads were lowered; a woman sighed.

Maherha looked at Dajee sadly. She sobbed. Ren wiped his eyes.

"Heaven created the world but it forgot to make happiness. It was only when Chairman Mao came that he brought us happiness. He taught us to love our fraternal people. . . ." Shama continued. Young Erhbu, in an irrepressible voice, suddenly shouted, "We, the Yi and Han peoples, should sit round one hearth in peace and unity!"

"Yes, like sisters and brothers. . . ." someone added.

"Like the winnow and the fan. . . ." chimed in someone else.

Shama knew the time was ripe to come to the point.

"Our Han brother, Old Man Ren, has come for his daughter. What do you think should be done?"

Silence, more silence.

Suddenly Maherha stood up and went to Dajee, took her hand and in a warm affectionate voice said, "Go, my Dajee, go with your real *Ahda*. . . ."

Dajee regarded Maherha with tears in her eyes, "*Ahda!*"

"Go, Dajee, go!" said all the Yi people.

Ren stumbled over to her daughter and stroked her hair. "My Niuniu, bow to your *Ahda* and your sisters and brothers to bid them goodbye. We must go. . . ."

"*Ahda*, I'm going," said Dajee to Maherha. "But I'll come back to see you."

Ren unwrapped the cloth bundle he had brought and took out a new blue cotton suit. "Change into this, child. You have not worn our clothes for a dozen years."

"Please, don't make Dajee change her costume," Maherha pleaded, gripping Ren's hands. "Please don't. I made these clothes for her with loving hands and heart.

She loves this pleated skirt, the beads and the head kerchief. . . ."

To Dajee, he said, "Go in these clothes and beads, my Dajee. When you see the costume in the future you'll remember how I endured the master's whip for you and how I warmed you on winter nights. When you see the beads, you'll remember the blood and tears I shed for you. . . . I'll be all alone when you are gone. . . ."

"I'll think of you every day," said Dajee, interrupting him, "and dream of you every night. . . ."

Maherha did not reply but turned to Ren. "I'm sure you'll love Dajee more than I. You must be good to her. She is fond of buckwheat flapjacks, you must remember to buy buckwheat flour for her. She loves beads, you must buy her new ones. She likes Yi songs, please don't stop her from singing them. When she does wrong, don't shout at her; there are as many scars on her young heart as on her body. . . ."

Dajee flung herself in Maherha's arms and broke into loud sobs against his hollow chest. Old Maherha kissed his daughter's hair with shrivelled lips.

Old Man Ren stood still, his eyes closed. I was afraid he would faint.

There was silence again. . . . Time seemed to have stopped.

After an endless pause, Ren dropped the blue cotton suit and rubbed his eyes.

"Child, you must remain here," he said finally, one hand on Maherha's arm and the other holding Dajee's. "Stay here with your *Abda*. I see now that he loves you more than I. I am your real father, but it was he who cared for you all these years. He did more for you than I. I have tasted enough of the sorrows of losing a daughter. My heart has already been torn; I cannot bear to see Grandad Maherha's heart torn the same way. I don't want to see him shed tears over a lost child. You must stay, my daughter...." Turning to Maherha, he said, "Old brother, I can die in peace, knowing that my daughter is in your hands."

Weeping, Dajee knelt down at Ren's feet and hugged his knees. "*Ahda*," she said between sobs, "I'm afraid I'll have to be a bad daughter to you. I've been here a dozen years, I've become one of the Liangshan people. I love *Ahda* Maherha, I love the people here, I cannot part from them. Together we suffered and groaned under the whip, together we wept and laughed...."

She raised her head to gaze at the rolling fields, her dark eyes shining. "Look, *Ahda*, isn't this a beautiful place? We have tall mountains, gurgling brooks, green maize, thick forests, and singing birds soaring in the sky. My father, your daughter will not forget you. I'll come to visit you regularly."

Maherha rushed up to Ren. Two pairs of thin but strong arms interlocked.

My heart seemed to have raced across the ridge of Liangshan Mountains, experiencing the very mood of nature — from misty gloom to radiant sunshine, from storm and wind to a boundless blue sky. I seemed to be in a dream, but no, it was all quite real.

Everyone's eyes were on the two old men, standing erect like stone figures. Their former differences and ill will forgotten, they stood close to each other, friends for ever:

"Let us drink!" cried Shama in a boisterous voice. "Go get some wine, Erhbu."

The crowd cheered.

Translated by Tang Sheng

Gao Ying was born in 1929 in Jiaozuo, Henan Province. He began to write poetry in Chongqing in 1945 and in the early fifties published The Song of Ding Youjun *and* Lamplights Around the Three Gorges, *the short story collection* High Mountains and Distant Rivers *and the novel* The Cloudy Cliff. *His short story* Dajee and Her Father, *which was made into a film, gained widespread attention.*

He is now deputy director of the editorial department of the Sichuan Broadcasting Station.

The Vegetable Seeds

Hao Ran

IT was nearly noon. In the canteen the steamed rolls were just ready. The cooks were busy preparing the dishes. Meng Zhaoxian, leader of the vegetable team, flitted into the courtyard, graceful and swift as a swallow.

A girl of nineteen, tall and slender, she had an oval face, a pair of limpid eyes and fine arched eyebrows. Her long plait, tied with scarlet wool, swung on her back as she walked, adding to her lively and vivacious air. Her face flushed, her forehead and nose beaded with perspiration, she came up to Aunt Meng who was chopping squash. "Any letters for me, ma?" she asked, breathing short.

Before her mother could answer, the other women giggled. Zhaoxian laughed happily, seizing her mother's arm. "Give it me, ma, quick," she urged. "I'm sure there's a letter."

Aunt Meng glared at her in mock anger. "They're laughing because you're such a crazy girl, always in a rush. Letters! Who's sending you a letter?"

Zhaoxian pouted. After a pause she asked, "Has the postman been? He comes here for a drink every time he passes our village. Have you seen him today?"

"No, I haven't, Zhaoxian, don't. . . ." But her daughter had flitted out again. She sighed.

Third Sister Meng, who was washing vegetables, looked at the departing figure of Zhaoxian and smiled. "I never knew your daughter had a boyfriend," she said to Aunt Meng. "But since she came back from buying vegetable seeds at the fair, she's been restless, waiting anxiously for a letter."

"Zhaoxian is a smart girl," put in Aunt Li. "You don't have to worry; she's sure to find you a good son-in-law."

Aunt Meng listened complacently to her neighbours' comments. It was only natural for a mother to think about her daughter's marriage. In the case of Zhaoxian, her mother did not have much to worry about because she knew the girl was sensible. But during the last few days the girl had lost her appetite and was not sleeping well. Her mother felt rather put out, rather angry with that man too. Why didn't he write? Why should he make her child unhappy? Today Zhaoxian seemed even more anxious. Unable to contain herself, Aunt Meng went to the gate and looked outside. The girl was again standing by the pond waiting for the postman. Her mother sighed.

In the shade of the willow beside the pond, Zhaoxian fixed her anxious eyes on the path which ran westward through the sorghum fields. How she hoped that a green bicycle would appear and stop before her, bringing her a pile of letters. Her eyes sore with straining, she waited and watched in vain. She counted on her fingers: One day, two days . . . already five days! Five days ago she had done something she thought very clever. That day she had gone to the fair at Baozhuang

Village to buy vegetable seeds, but once again she failed to get any. Since every people's commune was expanding its vegetable plot, seeds were in great demand. Without seeds their plan for a bumper harvest would be empty talk. Zhaoxian, clever and capable girl that she was, bought a sheet of red paper and borrowed a brush and inkstone from the primary school to write two copies of this "notice":

> To all production brigade leaders:
> In response to the directive of the Central Committee of the Party and the State Council, our production brigade wants to expand the area sown with autumn vegetables. But we haven't enough seeds. The commune has provided half the seeds we need; the other half we still lack. All our attempts to buy seeds so far have failed. Now we want to enlist your help. If you have any surplus seeds, whatever the amount, please write to us and we shall immediately come to buy them. Thanks in advance.
>
> Meng Zhaoxian,
leader of the vegetable team of
Mengjiatan Production Brigade

She pasted a copy of this notice at each end of the main street of Baozhuang, then walked home well satisfied, sure that this would get better, quicker results than scouring the countryside or telephoning round to make inquiries. As soon as she got home she asked her father, who was the brigade leader, to give them an additional ten *mu* for vegetables besides the original ten *mu*.

"You young people don't seem to know how to run things properly," remarked her father, none too pleased. "How can you plan production like that? You haven't got your seeds yet, but you want the land to wait for you. You know it is already sowing time. Seven days from now it will be too late to sow. Will you be responsible if that land lies idle?"

"Give me seven days then. If no letters come in time, you can sow your buckwheat." The girl was full of confidence.

Now already five days had passed — slowly yet all too quickly. On tenterhooks, she had lost her appetite. She did not sleep soundly either. For several nights she dreamed she was shouldering a sack of seeds and woke laughing, her fists clenched. The production brigade planned to provide each member with 500 catties of vegetables for the winter and spring. This was no light task. The girl felt she should not let the members down; she must carry out the plan. But whether or not this was feasible depended on these few days. Time waits for no man. And still the wretched postman had not come!

Cursing inwardly, she looked up and realized that it was past noon. The postman must have come and gone. Perhaps somebody had taken her letters to the brigade office. She hurried to the office only to find it locked, which made her fulminate inwardly against the old accountant who must have locked it. Then she leaned against the window-sill and looked through the gauze netting. The next instant she started for joy, like a traveller lost in the dark who suddenly glimpses a red lantern ahead. On the desk she saw four parcels addressed to her. What a windfall. In her excitement she drummed on the door. She thought of going to fetch the old accountant but was too impatient to waste so much time. Pacing the courtyard she soon hit on a way. She climbed on to the window-sill and tearing loose the gauze jumped in through the window. Grasping the four parcels, she jumped out, fixed the gauze in place again, then ran straight off towards the vegetable plot.

The parcels were heavy but she laughed to herself as she ran. After a while she slowed down and opened one. It was filled with purple-black seeds. The enclosed letter said: "We have not many seeds left and are sorry that we can only send you one catty. — Huadu Production Brigade of Tangwu Commune." She opened another parcel and the note inside said, "I was keeping this half catty of seeds for my private plot; but since your production brigade is in want of seeds, I send them to you. The collective should come before the individual. Don't worry about my plot which is only one-fifth of a *mu*, my neighbours will let me have some seedlings. . . ."

Her eyes misty, the girl pressed the four parcels to her heart, moved by the comradeliness behind these gifts.

As she walked on immersed in happy thoughts, a splashing was heard ahead and from a cluster of reeds emerged a man.

Once clear of the reeds he laid his package on the small stone bridge and, holding on to a willow with one hand, washed his muddy feet in the stream. Then he put on his shoes. The laces were not yet tied when he saw Zhaoxian. "Hey, comrade, is this Mengjiatan Village?" he asked loudly.

When she was in a happy mood Zhaoxian was inclined to like everybody she met and to enjoy a pleasant chat. "Yes, it's Mengjiatan," she replied smiling. "Where are you from? Visiting some relative here?"

The young man was tall and slim, with a broad forehead, a square jaw and lively, sparkling eyes. His blue cotton trouser-legs were rolled up, showing muscular legs. His white shirt was unbuttoned, revealing a white vest with the radiant red character "Award" in the middle. Below in smaller characters was printed: "From the headquarters of Jiashan Reservoir Project." This made the girl eye the stranger with respect. "I have no relatives here," the young man replied. "I'm looking for somebody. Can you tell me where Comrade Meng Zhaoxian of the vegetable team lives?"

"Looking for me?"

The young man smiled, revealing even white teeth. He stepped forward and said warmly, "So you are Comrade Meng. What a coincidence!"

"But . . . I don't know you," said the girl doubtfully.

"I come from the Leap Forward Commune of Anqiu County, south of the river," the young man said in a straightforward, friendly way. "My name is Wang Yuanqing. I've brought you some vegetable seeds."

Zhaoxian was startled. Anqiu County and Changle County to which her commune belonged were divided by the Wen River. The Leap Forward Commune and Mengjiatan Village were more than thirty *li* apart. How had he known they were short of vegetable seeds? And fancy him coming all this way to deliver them! Too grateful for words, she picked up the young man's package. "Must have caused you a lot of trouble. How can we thank you enough?" she murmured. The package was very heavy. "How much did you sow? How is it that you have so much to spare?" she asked.

"The other day I crossed the river to your county to learn Jaoya Commune's method of making chemical fertilizer. I passed by Baozhuang and saw your notice. When I went back I told our brigade leader about it. He immediately asked the storeman to see what seeds we had left to send to you. It turned out that all our surplus seeds had already been given to other communes. I knew you must be pretty desperate, otherwise you wouldn't have put up that notice. So I made the round of all our commune members and collected a handful of seeds here, another there. I got a little over ten catties."

The young man narrated this as if it were the most natural thing in the world. But Zhaoxian knew the distance he must have walked, going from house to house to collect these seeds, the many anxious appeals he must have made, the sweat it must have cost him. "You took such pains for us," she said. "You could have written, or mailed the seeds to us. But you went to the trouble to come yourself."

"Yes, I intended to mail them to you, but our brigade leader said he had been to your village and knew you didn't have much experience in growing vegetables. He gave me two days to deliver the seeds and discuss with you how best to sow them."

This was even more wonderful! Zhaoxian clapped her hands for joy. "I declare, you think of everything," she exclaimed. "That had me worried. Our vegetable team has only just been formed and I've got to learn from scratch. You must be an expert in raising vegetables;

please be my teacher. Come, let's go to the village first to have a rest."

The girl's warm praise embarrassed the young man who blushed. "I don't need a rest," he said. "Let's go to your vegetable plot. I'll have to start home early tomorrow morning."

"Even if you don't want to rest, you must eat something. Don't stand on ceremony. Come on."

"I won't turn down a meal," said the young man. "But first let's have a look at the vegetable plot so that we can discuss matters when we eat."

Zhaoxian nodded. Here was a man who knew how to make the best use of his time.

The two of them made directly for the vegetable plot, talking as they hurried along. Just then Aunt Meng appeared from the other end of the reeds. A basket filled with steamed rolls on her arm, she had come from the canteen to fetch her daughter home for lunch from the vegetable plot. Pleasantly surprised to come upon the girl with a young man, she returned to the canteen to buy more rolls. Then she made for the brigade office.

The old brigade leader and the old accountant had just returned from the fields. The accountant was fumbling for the key to open the office door. Aunt Meng hurried up to her old man, beaming, and said, "Come home, quick. Hurry!" Without waiting for his reply, she put down the basket and brushed the dust from his clothes. "Look at you, all over dust. People will laugh. It's nothing if they laugh at you, but they'll think my daughter and me bad managers."

Puzzled by this sudden excess of solicitude, the old

brigade leader pulled a long face and demanded, "What's all this fuss about? What's happened?"

"Just fancy! The letter didn't come but he's come instead," Aunt Meng remarked gleefully.

"Who's come?" asked her husband, still at a loss.

The old accountant clapped his hands and chuckled. "We're going to have a wedding feast. It must be Zhaoxian's young man."

"Impossible. First I've heard of it." The brigade leader shook his head.

"If she didn't even tell her ma, of course she won't have mentioned it to you," his wife said impatiently. "He's already sitting in our house, and you are still in the dark!"

They hurried home. Zhaoxian had just fetched the guest a basin of hot water.

"Here are my father and mother. My father's the head of our production brigade," Zhaoxian told the young man. And turning to her parents she said, "This is Comrade Wang Yuanqing from south of the river. . . ."

"Fancy my meeting you for the first time today. Why don't you drop in more often?" put in the girl's mother.

"This is the first time we've met too," Zhaoxian said. She went on to explain how Wang had come to help them.

Her mother was taken aback and her face burned. She was disappointed at first. Then, impressed by the story, she smiled.

The brigade leader shot his wife a quizzical glance and then invited the guest to join them at lunch. During the meal he expressed his gratitude to Wang and asked how things were doing south of the river. But Aunt

Meng managed to slip in a whole series of questions about young Wang's age, his family and so forth. When he told her that he and old mother lived alone, she smiled. "Your mother is a lucky woman, having such a progressive and able son as you." She helped Wang to another large steamed roll.

The people of Mengjiatan were greatly stirred and heartened by the help they were receiving from all sides. That afternoon, the brigade leader sent more than twenty members from other teams to help the vegetable team with its sowing. Wang Yuanqing acted as their technical adviser.

The young man was as active on the vegetable plot as if he were in his own production brigade. At the very start he made an important proposal — to sow in furrows or drills instead of scattering the seed broadcast. The result was that the seeds went twice as far and ten more *mu* of land were sown. This alone greatly impressed the villagers, especially Zhaoxian who was so eager to learn that she never left young Wang's side. She watched his hands, memorized his every movement, making him demonstrate how to sow and acting as his assistant. The young man worked systematically and deftly. The seeds were evenly spaced out and covered uniformly and smoothly with soil. Not only Zhaoxian, but all the commune members, acclaimed his skill.

Half a day and a night passed, and early the next morning Wang Yuanqing took his leave. The brigade leader and members of the vegetable team saw him out of the village, reluctant to part with him. And there was no sign of Zhaoxian's usual vivacity as she walked silently with young Wang to the river. There she grasped his hand and said, "How can we ever thank you, Comrade Yuanqing?"

The young man looked at the girl and suddenly blushed. "No need to thank me. I hope you will raise fine cabbages and turnips. That will be the best way to thank us."

Zhaoxian raised her head and said firmly, "Yes, I promise we will. But I hope you'll come back in the autumn, to see our crop for yourself."

The young man took off his shoes and forded the river. The girl followed him with her eyes, waving. As she watched his receding figure, a profoundly sweet sensation flooded her heart. Besides bringing them seeds and technical know-how, he had made an unforgettable impression on her, one she found it impossible to put into words.

Suddenly her mother came running up shouting, "Stop him! He's left his seed bag behind."

Zhaoxian took the bag from her mother. "Don't call him," she said mischievously. "He'll come again in the autumn. If he doesn't, I'll take it to him."

August 1960

Translated by Zhang Su

Hao Ran was born in 1932 in Jixian County, Hebei Province. His first short story Honeymoon *was published in 1956 and eight collections of short stories later appeared. Two of his novels,* Bright Skies *and* The Golden Road, *were made into films.*

He has also published three collections of essays and seven books of children's stories.

He is now a member of the Beijing branch of the Chinese Writers' Association, and a deputy to the Eighth Beijing People's Congress.

Long Distance Runner

Malqinhu

MOUNTED on a fine white horse long and graceful as a heron, Dukar rode slowly down from the southern hills. Returning to your native parts is like coming back to your mother. It makes you young, a child. Dukar was thirty-seven, rather "old" for an athlete. But today he felt as frisky as a young mountain goat. His grey tunic and trousers, bleached white by many washings, were simple and clean. The wide collar of his maroon sports shirt he wore rakishly outside the tunic. He had an urge to sing a local tune but, like many long distance runners, his voice was poor.

"We sing with our hearts," he quipped to himself, and grinned.

How well he knew this flower-bedecked grassland, the gorgeous constantly changing sunset clouds, the wind-eroded boulders by the roadside. How he loved the waves of grass like green satin, the quiet paths, the fragrance of the wild flowers growing in limitless profusion. . . .

The success of the local people's commune also stirred him. In fact he was on his way to a big commune

festival in celebration of a very good year.   In addition
to the usual entertainment, this year they were holding
a track meet.   The elders of his old home area had said:
"Let Dukar join the race.   Though he's become famous
outside, he's still a son of the herdsmen.   We want to
see whether he runs faster than he did as a boy, or
slower."   The Communist Party committee of the
herdsmen's commune had sent him a warm invitation by
telegraph and he had enthusiastically accepted.

Rounding a few hillocks, the white horse entered upon
a grassy plain.   In the centre stood a single big elm,
popularly known as "Lovers' Tree".   It was a favourite
trysting place for sweethearts.   Sometimes, for privacy's
sake, a couple would climb up into its branches where
they whispered words of love amid its dense foliage.
First, however, they always rested a man's lassoing pole
against the tree trunk, or hung a girl's kerchief on a
lower branch, to show that the elm was "occupied".
Then no one else intruded.

Dukar had never made love here, but every time he
passed in summer he halted to enjoy the shade.   And
so today, he thought he'd stop a while too.   But as he
headed for the tree a strange sight caught his eye. About
a dozen boys appeared on the plain. They were running
behind another young fellow on a horse.   What were
they doing — chasing something?   Why didn't the boy
on the horse race ahead?   Why did he keep looking back
at them over his shoulder?   Was it some kind of a game?
Then why weren't they laughing and shouting?

Curious, Dukar clapped his legs against his animal's
sides and trotted towards them.   When he was a short
distance away, he reined in and shouted a greeting to
the sweating boys:

"How are you, neighbours!"

The boys were around sixteen or seventeen, which meant they were only a year or two old when Dukar had left home. A few perhaps hadn't even been born. Naturally they didn't recognize him, and his call of "neighbours" made no impression upon them. As they ran past, they only gave him a glance. None of them replied with the traditional courtesy of the herdsman.

Dukar didn't feel disappointed. He guessed that they were practising long distance running. To check on his surmise, he cantered his horse till he caught up with the boy in the rear — a yellow-haired youngster — and asked:

"Training for a long distance run?"

He could see that the boy was working hard — "fighting fatigue" as the athletes say. The boy nodded.

And the lad on the horse — was he the trainer? Dukar wanted to ask the yellow-haired boy, but didn't because he was obviously straining so.

When they were four or five hundred metres from Lovers' Tree the boy on the horse rose in his stirrups and turned around. Waving his hand, he yelled:

"Ready, go!"

At this signal, the runners raced forward for all they were worth.

Lovers' Tree evidently was their destination. When they got there, they jogged around on the grass to cool off. That was when Dukar caught up. Checking his horse, he shouted:

"Hello, athletes!"

The greeting sounded strange to the youngsters, but they replied and came towards him. A few halted directly in front of him.

"Don't stop yet." Dukar clapped one of the boys on the shoulder. "Walk it off."

The boy on the horse rode over. "Where are you from, comrade?"

"Hohhot."

"Where you heading?"

"Right here."

"To our village?"

Dukar nodded. He asked: "Practising long distance running?"

"Yes. We're the amateur team of the Lovers' Tree People's Commune. Thirteen of us altogether. Say, comrade, where do you work?"

Dukar didn't want to reveal his identity too soon. He parried the question:

"I suppose you're the trainer?"

The lad grinned. Turning to his mates, he shouted:

"This comrade says I'm your trainer. You'd better listen to me from now on!"

The boys roared with laughter. They slowly congregated under Lovers' Tree.

Dukar was delighted with the young fellows. Tying his horse to a boulder, he walked up to them and said:

"You're fine runners. You're as fast as the antelope."

"We're not much. There are others who run much faster!" the yellow-haired youngster replied with a sniff. He had a round baby face.

"Little Tow Head is right. We just run along behind for the practice," another boy chimed in.

"Who runs faster than you fellows?"

"Well, there's Dukar in Hohhot, if you're talking about far from here. He's a champion, broke the national record three times. Teaches long distance running in the Athletic Academy of Inner Mongolia. Used to be our neighbour when he was small. Light brown eyes, curly hair, runs like the wind. . . ."

Little Tow Head spoke with much dramatic intensity in his desire to convince his auditor. His face was full of emotion and he gestured vigorously with his two small hands like a veteran actor. He was an adorable kid.

Dukar suppressed a smile. "Never mind far away. What about here?"

"Here, we have Djimed. . . ."

Dukar looked around at the other boys.

"Which one is he?"

"He's gone to a meeting of our commune's Communist Youth League committee. He's one of our committee members."

"You Hohhot people don't know anything. Haven't you even heard of Djimed?" Little Tow Head shook his mop of yellow hair reproachfully. "He's our best long distance runner. You couldn't keep up with him on a three-year-old horse. He's also our neighbour."

Dukar could restrain himself no longer. Chuckling, he said in a provocative tone:

"I'd like to race against him, Little Tow Head."

The lad looked him over from head to foot. "You?" he retorted loftily. "You might keep up — if you rode that horse of yours!"

The other boys burst out laughing. Dukar really loved that kid! How clever he was! The little devil may be exaggerating a bit, thought Dukar, but Djimed is probably a very good runner.

"And I suppose it was you who developed Djimed,

Comrade Trainer," Dukar said to the boy who had been riding the horse.

"I'm not the trainer. We all take turns riding, a different one of us each day."

"What use is riding a horse to long distance running?"

"When you chase after a horse, you learn to run fast."

"Oh? Who says so?"

"That's been the experience of Champion Dukar," inserted Little Tow Head before the other boy could answer.

"I know Dukar very well, but I never heard him say anything like that," replied Dukar, half in jest.

"It's absolutely true. Anyone around here over thirty will tell you." All the boys echoed Little Tow Head's assertion.

More confident than ever, the youngster explained: "When Uncle Dukar was little, he used to run behind his lord's horse all day. That's why we also. . . ."

Dukar didn't know why the boy's words should disturb him so. A lump rose in his throat, he shivered slightly.

"You don't understand Dukar!" he cried.

He was sorry at once that he had let himself be so agitated. His sudden shout had startled the boys. They looked at him in alarm. To break the awkward pause he addressed them with warmth and affection after regaining his composure.

"A long distance runner doesn't necessarily have to run behind a horse, kids. Though Dukar did it when he was small, you don't think it was because he wanted to, do you?"

To calm the turmoil in his heart, he fell silent. His mind went back to his unhappy past.

When he was eight years old, he was given as a slave to the local lord. Because he was a clever hard-working child, the lord had him make tea and serve food, and took him wherever he went. The lord was a cruel swine. If Dukar displeased him in the slightest, he beat him with a whip. The child's body was covered with scars from one year to the next.

One day, Dukar was again whipped for no reason. Already a boy of fifteen, he could no longer endure this beastly existence. He decided to run away from the grassland and seek a place where people lived like human beings. One silent night, he stealthily led out the lord's white steed. As he was about to mount, gongs sounded and people began to shout. He had been discovered by the night watchman. In his haste Dukar lost his direction and ran blindly. He was caught in the end and taken back to the lord.

The lord beat him cruelly, "You cheeky bastard! So you don't want to be a slave, eh?" shouted the lord. "I'll show you!"

For "running away from his master" Dukar was forbidden ever to ride again.

Thereafter, Dukar suffered even worse. The lord still took him along when he went abroad, but now Dukar, not permitted to ride, had to run behind his master's horse. Whether wind or rain or snow or fog, whether broiling summer or frigid winter, while the lord galloped ahead Dukar raced after him, never lagging a step. Sometimes Dukar had no shoes, and he ran barefoot, his soles cracking and staining the road with blood. Sometimes he gasped for breath and spit blood, but he was determined not to beg for mercy. No matter how he suffered, he just angrily clenched his teeth.

It was the intention of the black-hearted lord to kill him slowly in this way, but Dukar saw through his scheme and took measures to defend himself. He began paying attention to the technique of running. He learned to utilize his energy, to plan his speed. Thus, as the years went by, he mastered the art of long distance running. A few dozen *li* a day meant nothing to him. Not only didn't the master run him to death, on the contrary, he turned Dukar into a man of iron. By the time the master discovered his mistake, the end of his lording it over the people was fast approaching. Before long, the area was liberated, and Dukar joined a cavalry unit of the people's army. . . .

As he recalled this, a smile came to Dukar's face. Rising to his feet, he gazed up at the sunset clouds and heaved a long comfortable sigh. He took off his cap and wiped the sweat from his forehead with it. His curly brown hair was tousled like a chrysanthemum. Unbuttoning his tunic to let some of the evening breeze in, he exposed his maroon sport shirt. The words 'Inner Mongolia" were written on it in Mongolian and Chinese. Little Tow Head was the first to spot them. Pressing his right index finger to his lower lip, he exclaimed joyously:

"You're also an athlete?"

"That's right."

"Are you a track man or a ball player?" the tallest of the boys inquired.

As Dukar was about to answer, Little Tow Head jumped and let out a yell like he'd discovered a new continent.

"He's Uncle Dukar, fellows! Look at his curly hair, his light brown eyes!"

"It *is* Uncle Dukar. He's exactly the same as his picture in the magazines!"

But when the boys discovered that standing before them was really and truly Dukar the champion athlete, they were embarrassed. Their mischievous grins, their noisy shouts were gone, as if blown away by the cool evening breeze, leaving in their place only astonished stares. Dukar understood these country kids. They had seen little of the outside world. They weren't being unfriendly. On the contrary, they were longing to establish a friendly atmosphere as quickly as possible. Dukar told them not to train by running behind a horse any more. With a few funny remarks he soon had them laughing, and they were their lively selves again.

That was how champion athlete Dukar and the future champion athletes from his native parts became acquainted.

During the three days since his return home Dukar, in keeping with the customs of the herdsmen, visited all the elders of the village. Old men gave him their blessings. Old women, tears in their eyes, kissed him on the forehead. For Dukar, who had been orphaned by the cruel society that had been deposed, it was like being bathed in a sea of warmth and affection. Accompanied by friends of his childhood — among them the present secretary of the commune's Communist Party committee — he visited the commune's pastures, its primary schools, its dairy, its small hydro-electric station. The old place had become as youthful as a bridegroom. Of course during those three days much of his time was taken up by the young long distance runners. From the first thing in the morning until twilight's fall, they surrounded him, leaving reluctantly only when called home for their evening tea.

Dukar went to bed early, for tomorrow was the first day of the big festival, and he wanted to be well rested for the race. But he couldn't fall asleep. Lying in the yurt where he had been born and raised, he gazed through the smoke vent on top at the dark blue sky and the twinkling stars. He thought of himself, of the new generation, his relatives and friends, and of the Communist Party that was a million times brighter than the sun. . . . It was very late at night, when the festival eve singing of the women was stilled, that he slept at last, smiling like a baby gorged with its mother's milk.

The next morning everything was drenched in gold — the grasslands, the forests, the hills and lakes.

Ah, a lovely day that no money could buy!

Steeped in the pleasure of a good harvest and the joy of festival time, the herders, young and old, singing and dancing, came from all over to the beautifully decorated fair grounds.

The tournament began. Horse races, archery contests, wrestling matches, evoked no end of cheers and enthusiastic shouts. The grasslands were a sea of merriment. Every stone, every blade of grass, every grain of sand, seemed to be laughing.

The cross-country race was about to start. This was something new to the herders, and they watched with interest, much heightened of course by the arrival of Dukar.

All the other competitions of that day had now ended. The voice over the loudspeaker began announcing the long distance race. The announcer also relating Dukar's victories in races at home and abroad. Dukar hated to have anyone praise him. As the Mongolian folk saying goes: The pretty girl dislikes nothing more than people pinning flowers in her hair. A compliment made him blush to the ears; he was afraid to raise his head. Seeing this, the old folks were pleased. "Dukar hasn't lost his herdsman's modesty," they said to one another.

Dukar entered the grounds and began warming up, avoiding any movements that might strike the local people as strange. He merely trotted back and forth to loosen his legs and mid-section. Then he walked off to the sidelines.

The crowd let out a cheer, for the young fellows he was going to race against had just come on to the field. Dressed in red sleeveless jerseys, white shorts and white sneakers, they looked smart and fit. Dukar gazed at them admiringly.

Interestingly enough, the people wished the runners luck in the ancient ceremonial manner ordinarily used for wrestlers. Each boy was lifted up by several herdsmen, who sang him a paean of encouragement and praise.

The herdsmen near Dukar also raised him up and, when they finished singing their felicitations, pushed him into the field. He and the young contestants looked each other over. Not less than twenty were taking part in the race. Little Tow Head as always was the liveliest of the lot. Dukar looked for the Djimed the boys had spoken so highly of. Djimed had been away at a meeting the last few days, and Dukar hadn't seen him. Just then, chattering like a spring swallow, Little Tow Head half pulled and half pushed a young fellow of eighteen or nineteen towards him. Slim-waisted, shy, he didn't

look like a long distance runner. But since Dukar
hadn't met this boy before, he guessed he must be
Djimed. Walking over to him, Dukar asked:

"Are you Djimed?"

"We all call him Little Dukar. You're right. He is
Djimed," the quick-witted, fast-talking Little Tow
Head asserted.

Dukar put a friendly arm over Djimed's shoulders.
"Little Tow Head tells me you can run like the wind."

Djimed had the same failing as Dukar. Whenever
anyone praised him, his face and ears turned red and
he didn't know what to do with his hands and feet.
Hanging his head, he smiled but didn't speak. Actually,
he had been longing to talk with Dukar. But now that
they had finally met, perhaps because he was over-
excited, he couldn't say a word.

"See what a lot of neighbours have come today,
Djimed. You've got to show them some real running!"
Dukar encouraged him.

Djimed only gave a murmur of assent, his lower lip
between his teeth. But this told Dukar more than a
hundred words, there was such strength and determination behind it!

The loudspeaker called for the runners to take their
places. Dukar and the twenty others bunched at the
starting line. He glanced at Djimed. The boy stood
behind several others, as if afraid of being seen. He
was practically the last one to start when the gun went
off.

There was no measured distance for the race. Whoever reached Lovers' Tree, touched it and came back
first would be the winner. It must be at least ten
thousand metres altogether, Dukar thought.

The cheers of the crowd faded behind them as the contestants left the field and began the long difficult run.

While it was hardly likely that any among them was a match for Dukar, as in any regular race, he carefully planned his speed for each stage.

At first, the boys' pace was very fast. Dukar ran eighth or ninth. He knew they couldn't keep it up for long, and so was in no hurry to pass them. Sure enough, after they had gone about a thousand metres, they began spreading out. Dukar counted. He was still six men behind. Even Little Tow Head was ahead of him. Dukar increased his pace a bit and passed the boy. Little Tow Head had been looking rather proud of himself because he was running ahead of the champ. As Dukar passed him, he tugged the boy's sunflower-coloured hair and gestured to him encouragingly. But the lad didn't respond — perhaps he hadn't the strength to go any faster — and Dukar left him behind.

The boys in the lead showed no signs of slackening. Djimed was first, and he did indeed "run like the wind". It was plain he had plenty of power in his legs, but he didn't swing his arms properly, and this gave his movements a somewhat strained appearance.

His old surroundings kept bringing back waves of recollections to Dukar. This grassy field, this very path — how many times his running feet pounded it fifteen years ago. He had led an animal's existence in those days of blood and tears. . . . Never would he have believed then that fifteen years hence he would be racing across this same turf in very different circumstances.

Suddenly a young fellow passed him from behind.

Dukar looked ahead. The boys in the lead were out-distancing him by at least fifty metres. He had become so immersed in his memories that he had slowed his pace. Dukar took hold of himself. He couldn't let the lead become any larger. Steadily, rhythmically, he ran on.

When they were about five hundred metres from Lovers' Tree, the boys up front began putting on speed, probably wanting to increase their lead as much as possible before the first half of the race was completed. The leaders were bunched together, pacing themselves entirely on Djimed. Although this was a friendly competition, the boys took it very seriously. They seemed to have planned their strategy in advance. Dukar remembered what the neighbours had told him — Young Djimed has got brains in his head.

He decided to test the boy's staying-power in a sprint. Increasing his speed, he gained on them step by step. He soon shortened the distance between them. When the leaders heard his rapid steps coming closer, they scooted like a bunch of scared rabbits. Only Djimed remained calm. "Take it easy, take it easy," he reminded them.

As they neared Lovers' Tree, every one of them, Dukar included, seemed to forget that half the race still lay ahead. All drove to take the lead. The competition was white hot.

Djimed was the first to touch Lovers' Tree, followed immediately by several other young fellows. Dukar was fifth. Without a pause he turned and took after them. The leaders wouldn't give an inch. They maintained their positions for another four or five hundred metres. Then several of the boys, weakening under the veteran's pressure, began dropping back — one pace, then a second, until they were a good distance behind the leader, and Dukar passed them easily. Soon, only Djimed remained ahead of him. The youngster showed not a trace of fatigue. His stride was as quick and firm as ever.

Dukar had expended quite a bit of strength in that sprint. Conserving his energy for the final dash, he didn't try to overtake Djimed. Instead, slowing his pace slightly, he kept twenty to thirty metres between them.

But Djimed was determined to shake him off. Not only didn't he slow down — he increased his speed. Before long, he had left Dukar fifty metres behind. Dukar, sure Djimed couldn't maintain the pace, made no attempt to narrow the gap.

Djimed drove on relentlessly. Dukar was now two hundred metres to his rear. They had covered about seven thousand metres by then. Djimed still hadn't slackened. Even if he couldn't muster a dash at the end, just to have run seven thousand metres at this pace was in itself quite remarkable. Dukar began to admire the boy's endurance and speed.

Years of experience told him that this was the crucial part of the race. Concentrating his energies, he stepped up his stride. Gradually, he shortened the distance between them. But he had to pay a big price for every step. By the time he was fifty metres to Djimed's rear, he was assailed by the athlete's most fearful opponent — fatigue. Dukar was growing more and more tired.

He looked at Djimed. How much push the boy had! Dukar couldn't let up a single stride. In his mind there was only one thought: Catch him! Catch him!

The veteran runner pursued like the wind, the young

athlete sped like lightning. To tell the truth, Dukar had never been so subject to an opponent's initiative as he was today. He was like a novice, his plan completely disrupted. Whether he speeded up or slowed down depended entirely on the other fellow's whim. But he had no time to think about such matters now. He clung to just one idea: Hang on!

The fair grounds were vaguely visible in the distance. That meant they now were entering the home stretch. As of this moment, the champion hadn't once passed his rival. Maybe this new athlete would defeat him. From the look of things, it was quite possible.

In an attempt to save the situation, Dukar began his last dash while still more than a thousand metres from the finish line. Djimed at once returned the compliment. Although the gap between them was plainly narrowing, because Dukar had not handled his changes of pace well and wasted too much strength in over-zealous spurts, now at this critical juncture he had no reserves left to call upon. He was visibly weakening.

With only five hundred metres to go, Dukar was still twenty metres behind.

He could already faintly hear the cheers of the crowd.

They were on the home stretch.

Fatigue, heavy as the wind-eroded boulders by the roadside, pressed down on his body. How he would wipe out that long, long twenty-metre lead, he had no idea. Judging from previous races, under such conditions there was only a ten to one chance that he might win. Defeat was an unpleasantness an athlete met many times in his lifetime. But defeat was the very thing that helped many young newcomers become good athletes, and good athletes become better. . . . Dukar had lost many times, but now he felt he must win. He had no alternative!

Dukar knew what a deep impression a first contest made on a new athlete. Djimed unquestionably was a brilliant runner. He had a splendid future ahead of him. But if he should beat a champion in his very first race, victory would seem too easy. It would influence him in subsequent competitions.

This thought seemed to inject Dukar with miraculous strength. His weariness vanished. In his mind there was but a single thought:

For his own sake, I've got to beat him!

Sure enough, he flew forward as if equipped with a new pair of legs. Metre after metre, the power generated from his heart let him gobble up the distance between them. . . .

He shot past Djimed. He was one metre ahead, two, three. . . .

As Dukar crossed the finishing line he was well over ten metres in the lead.

A moment later, Djimed also sped across. He ran up to Dukar and pantingly congratulated him:

"You ran the last stretch beautifully, Comrade Dukar!"

Holding back the words of praise that were on the tip of his tongue, Dukar only smiled and complimented Djimed indirectly.

"I never had to make such a dash. If this meet were being clocked, I probably would have broken the national record for the fourth time!"

He hugged young Djimed tightly in his big arms —

no, he embraced him with his whole heart. Two drops of moisture glistened in the corners of the veteran athlete's eyes. Who knows whether they were perspiration or tears of joy!

Translated by Sidney Shapiro

The Mongolian writer Malqinhu was born in 1930 in Tumd Banner, Liaoning Province. He joined the Communist-led Eighth Route Army and began to write reports and plays. 1951 saw the publication of his much-lauded first novel On the Kolchin Grasslands. *He has also published short story anthologies as well as the award-winning novel* The Barren Grasslands.

He now works as assistant editor of the magazine Nationalities Literature *and is vice-chairman of the Federation of Literary and Art Circles of the Mongolian Autonomous Region.*

Barley Kernel Gruel

Li Zhun

ALL was quiet at noonday in the sultry fields.

Not a breath of wind stirred the dropping leaves by the roadside. Clouds like fish-scales drifted lazily through the sky. The early June sun, beating down like fire on to the wheat, made the tips glow the ruddy gold of ripe apricots. The barley had been reaped, leaving nothing but silver stubble along the ridges.

Because of the heat and the fact that it was noon, there was not a soul on the land. Trees and crops drowsed sleepily. But from the ears of wheat in the terraced fields there wafted penetrating gusts of fragrance.

This was hilly country and a dirt track wound like a brown belt over the undulating landscape. Along this steep road two men were pushing a cart loaded with four telegraph poles of stout, straight red pine. The wheels of the cart were creaking.

The younger of the two men, Lei Wansheng, was a sturdy fellow in his early twenties. Sweat had gathered on the bushy eyebrows above his large black eyes, and he was panting for breath, his full red lips parted. He Suilin, his mate and senior by several years, looked the younger of the two. Short and light on his feet, he had small, rather boyish features, giving him the appearance of an overgrown child.

It was clear that they had come unprepared for this heat, for both were wearing long pants and thick shirts. Lei was sweating so much that the characters "Zhengzhou Electric Machine Works" printed in red on his shirt were sticking to his chest.

They were delivering these telegraph poles from Zhengzhou to White Goose Ridge Production Brigade. A month previously their foreman, Old Lu, had joined a work team sent to help the villages and had been assigned to this production brigade to install an electrically operated pump station. The brigade had prepared all the necessary wire, machinery and other equipment, but proved to be short of four telegraph poles, and these were not procurable on the spot, as the region produced nothing but deciduous trees. The local cadres brought along carrying poles used for sedan-chairs and old cross-beams, but none of these was the specified height or thickness. In the end, Old Lu wrote to his management asking them to help by sending some of the works' own stock of poles. Lei and He had been chosen to make the delivery.

This county lay not far from Zhengzhou, only two stops away by train. When they alighted at the station and learned that White Goose Ridge was just eighteen *li* away, Lei rolled up his sleeves and started off with the cart.

"Let's have a snack first," said He. "It's after eight."

But there was quite a crowd round the canteen and Lei, observing this, answered airily, "Come on! It's only eighteen *li*. We'll eat when we find Old Lu."

So the two of them set off with the telegraph poles. To

start with, they exchanged light-hearted comments on the probable yield of the wheat on both sides of the road, and the strength and stamina of donkeys, while young Lei enlivened their progress by his imitations of bird calls.

They covered a dozen *li* without stopping to rest. After crossing several ridges and climbing not a few steep hills, they suddenly found the road before them cut. A passer-by informed them that the commune was building a highway to White Goose Ridge and they would have to go round by Walnut Gully. When farmers give directions, instead of confining themselves to a simple "Turn left" or "Turn right" like city folk, they launch into detailed instructions like a mathematics teacher holding forth to his class. On the basis of what they were told He made a rapid mental calculation and realized that this detour would let them in for another eighteen *li*. One thing reassured them, however, and that was the news that after reaching Persimmon Valley in the east they could follow the telegraph poles to White Goose Ridge.

As they trundled the cart back the way they had come, young Lei's comments on the wheat and donkeys dried up. So did his bird calls. He plodded glumly along, too disgusted to take out his handkerchief, using his sleeves to mop his sweating face.

He knew just how he felt, and in an attempt to keep his spirits up hummed snatches of Henan opera — slightly off-key. Young Lei could sing Shaoxing opera but he kept silent, except for the rumbling of his empty stomach.

After toiling past a few more ridges and valleys, He lapsed into silence too. By now all the peasants had

left the fields and the sun was beating down more
fiercely than ever. The swish of the cart wheels through
the dust, punctuated by laboured breathing, was the
only sound on the highway.

In the distance two large, leafy walnut trees came
into sight, and just beyond them all telegraph poles
stretched into the distance. That put new life into both
men and with joyful shouts Lei shoved the cart up the
slope, beads of sweat pouring off him like rain dripping
into his eyes. But great was their disappointment at
the top! For there was nothing here but walnut trees,
not a single village or wayside stall in that empty, rolling country. They could see White Goose Ridge, true
enough, but one look at the line of telegraph poles
made it clear that it was at least ten *li* away and very
difficult going into the bargain.

Lei let go of the cart and squatted in the shade of
the trees. He refused to move.

"What's up?" asked He. "That's White Goose Ridge
ahead."

"I can't make it," Lei declared. "I've come over
dizzy."

Secretly amused, He joined him in the shade.

"Confound these blistering hills!" swore Lei. "Not
a snack bar or village to be seen, not even a river!"

"We ought to have bought a few buns at the station,"
said He.

Lei ignored this remark and, his eyes on the walnut
tree, asked, "When do walnuts ripen?"

"Not till autumn," He informed him. "It's no use
looking so hopeful — there's nothing but leaves."

Still Lei stared up at the trees. "I wish they were

loquats!" he sighed. "Where I come from this is just the time for loquats."

They rested a while in a dispirited silence, their eyes fixed on the cottages on the distant hill beyond which lay White Goose Ridge. In the shimmering sunlight the village, surrounded by trees, seemed like an oasis of clear green and turquoise blue, while the brooks and irrigation canals below interlaced each other like sparkling silver girdles. The cackling of hens carried faintly to their ears. Plumes of smoke curled up from the cluster of grey-tiled roofs to hover in the air.

This kitchen smoke caused Lei fresh pangs of hunger. And a bird, alighting at that moment on a bough above them, warbled a greeting which sounded for all the world like "Cuppa tea! Cuppa tea!" To young Lei, this was adding insult to injury. "Shut up, you!" he shouted. "We haven't even water to drink!" Both he and He burst out laughing.

Lei had barely stretched out in the shade, his hat over his face, when he caught the appetizing smell of food. Sitting up with a start, he saw a girl approaching by a path through the fields. She was wearing a new straw hat and blue check blouse, but from the waist down was hidden by the wheat. A few strands of glossy black hair lay over her temples, her cheeks were ruddy from exposure to the sun, and beads of perspiration had gathered at the tips of her finely arched eyebrows. The freckles on the bridge of her nose seemed vermilion in the sun. It was such a sweltering day that her liquid eyes seemed to be brimming over. In her left hand she carried a blue porcelain pitcher covered with a pea-green bowl, in her right hand a bamboo basket. Beneath the white towel on the basket was a big pile of onion cakes.

The heat drove this girl, too, into the shade of the trees, on the other side from the men. Sitting down with her back to them, she fanned herself with her straw hat, her bright, artless eyes fixed on the golden wheat.

The breeze she set up by her fanning wafted the smell of food still more tantalizingly into the men's faces. They identified the spicy savour of onion cakes and lettuce with green pepper and gelatin. In addition there was the aroma of some sort of gruel unlike anything that young Lei had experienced before, reminiscent of the scent of young wheat in the fields, its flavour heightened by cooking.

These appetizing odours made the men more conscious than ever of their hunger. With a glance at Lei, He suggested, "Suppose we move on?" He saw no point in staying there to be tormented.

Lei knew what he meant, for his own mouth was watering. "All right," he said. Then he turned to ask the girl, "How far is it, Elder Sister, to White Goose Ridge?"

The girl's finely chiselled lips curved in a smile at such a form of address from a bronzed, burly man. Shyly pointing to the hill ahead, she said, "Eight *li*. That red building beyond the stream is the brigade's new power station." Her voice was crisp, with the ringing tone of a bell.

"Your *li* in the mountains seems longer than on the plains," remarked young Lei.

"Yes, it's uphill and down dale all the way, so that eight *li* really amounts to well over ten." Only now did she turn to face them.

Their spirits rose at her air of concern. Young Lei seized the chance to say, "Oh, well, let's go. I could eat three big bowls of rice now, if only I had them!"

"What about pancakes?" asked He, deliberately.

"Pancakes? I could polish off ten!"

They watched the girl as they spoke, but she seemed not to have heard, judging by the lack of expression on her face. She was twiddling a wheat stalk and staring into the distance.

With a glance at his friend, Lei said rather sheepishly, "All right, get moving. No use talking about food here. I'd be thankful even for a sip of water."

"If you ignore the advice of your elders and betters, you're bound to run into trouble," declared He sententiously. "If you'd listened to me, you'd have eaten two big buns at the station and drunk some lentil gruel. Then you'd have more energy now."

Lei slapped his chest. "Well, missing a couple of meals isn't going to kill us. The Red Army crossed snowy mountains and fearful marshes — who's afraid of these little hills?" He tightened his belt, while the girl nibbled at her wheat stalk and smiled without saying a word.

"If we want to help the farmers, we mustn't mind hardships," continued Lei. "Didn't Old Lu say in his letter that once they have these poles eight hundred *mu* of dry land can be irrigated? Come on — let's put on a spurt!"

"That's all right with me." He grinned. "I'm not the one who's so hungry."

This last exchange had evidently set the girl thinking. She sprang to her feet and shyly yet firmly said, "If you're hungry, comrades, I've food here."

The two men hesitated and exchanged embarrassed glances.

"Go on!" she urged. "You've a steep climb ahead. And you're hauling a heavy load."

Her genuine sympathy overcame their scruples.

"Well, since Elder Sister's so good, let's have a snack, young Lei," suggested He. "No need to stand on ceremony."

"Right you are," agreed Lei, who was blushing like a boy.

The food was passed over. Onion cakes, a cold salad, and paper-thin pancakes made of fine white flour. The two men did not bother with vegetables: the pancakes disappeared down their throats like a flurry of snow-flakes.

While Lei was still eating, He and the girl started chatting.

"Is your wheat crop good this year?"

"The best for a very long time. We're planning to sell more grain to the state this year."

"Then the state will be able to produce more machines for you."

"That's right! Nowadays the workers in town are doing all they can for us in the country. Yesterday they brought back electric bulbs for our village — much bigger than the bulbs in electric torches! They'll soon be fixed up."

"Had you never seen electric light?"

"I've seen it at the film shows." She smiled naively. "Why, that big light throws the moon into the shade!"

Young Lei, still munching pancakes, casually rapped his chopsticks against the pitcher and said, "There are some as big as this."

The sound served as a reminder. The girl exclaimed, "Why, here am I chatting and forgetting to give you a drink." She made haste to fill a bowl for each of them.

Young Lei saw a gruel made from golden beans and some grain much larger than rice but considerably smaller than lotus seeds, which was floating like pearls in the bowl. He tasted a mouthful — it had a fresh, sweet flavour. It slipped smoothly over his tongue and down his gullet.

He drank three bowls to two of He's, and was going to help himself to a fourth when the girl flushed red as a maple leaf and protested in some confusion, "Comrade, leave a bit for someone working in our fields."

It cost her such an effort to get this out, you could almost hear her heart thumping. Lei felt abashed and He interposed, "That's quite enough. We've had plenty."

"Have some more pancakes!" urged the girl.

The men assured her they had eaten their fill and hastened to produce money.

"We don't take money, comrades, up here in the hills. You're welcome to a meal."

"That won't do! . . ." It was the men's first visit to the country and they continued to press payment on her, but were at a loss for words.

"No, really, comrades. This is nothing. I'm not a snack vendor!" She spoke gently and smiled, but they saw she was adamant. With sheepish thanks they set off with their cart.

After they had gone a fair way, young Lei remarked, "They're queer people hereabouts. She refused to accept any money, but she wouldn't give me another bowl of that gruel. Made me feel a regular fool."

"Must be someone waiting for her in the fields," said He.

"Well, I call it rather mean," rejoined young Lei. "If you offer a fellow food, you should let him fill his belly."

"Haven't you filled your belly?" retorted his friend. "You ate at least ten pancakes!"

"Maybe. But I wanted a few more bowls of that gruel."

They delivered the four poles to White Goose Ridge by the end of the noon siesta, and found Old Lu. The local cadres were so loud in their thanks that soon the news had spread through all the village. Old Lu found the two young men a place to rest. "Take it easy now," he said. "When you fix up the poles tomorrow, mind you don't take up good land or spoil the crops. And at meal times just you eat what the peasants give you. Don't say you fancy this or that. If you do, the folk here will go out of their way to produce it, and that's no good. When we come to the country, we must eat and live like the peasants." He looked so hard at Lei after this admonition that the young man stuck his tongue out in dismay. He had meant to ask what that gruel had been made of, but now he did not dare. Old Lu's word was law.

The next day dawned overcast and unusually fresh, with a light wind from the east. They set to work to fix up the electric wires. Lei climbed up a pole beside a big tree at the entrance to the village, and was so busy installing the porcelain insulators that when He walked past with a village cadre Lei did not trouble to call out a greeting, and He did not notice him.

Just then, from below, he heard a woman's voice which sounded strangely familiar.

"That man who just walked past is one of those who ate our lunch yesterday," said the girl. "There was a fat fellow with him who really tucked in, munching so lustily it was all I could do not to laugh."

Young Lei recognized that voice, clear as a bell, and took care not to make a sound.

A man replied, "You were mean not to let him eat his fill."

"How was I to know they were coming to fix up the electric lines for our village?"

"What difference did it make where they were going? You should have fed them properly. They've come down from their factory to help the villages."

"There'd have been nothing left for you in that case! You'd done a hard morning's work, so I took the trouble to make some barley kernel gruel for you. I'd have felt bad if you couldn't even taste it."

"Trust you to have an answer for everything! . . ." The man broke off, and the girl began to chuckle.

Lei, hugging the telegraph pole, dared not look down but he felt two pairs of eyes boring into his back.

When the time came for lunch, the chief of the production brigade sent He and Lei off with a young farm hand. He was a handsome fellow in his mid-twenties, with big, friendly eyes.

They followed him to his house in a small, clean courtyard. The gateway was newly built, and posted on the door was a wedding couplet:

> With men and women equal, work goes well,
> Free marriages are happy marriages.

The red paper had faded, but the writing still stood out clearly and could hardly date from earlier than January. A pomegranate tree in front of the gate was a mass of flame-red blooms. On the low coping round the tree stood two pots of garden balsam which country girls use to redden their finger-nails.

The young peasant led the way into the house, made He and Lei sit down at a well-scrubbed table and then went into the kitchen. He returned with a staggering pile of onion cakes, then brought in some big bowls of rice and two side dishes: scrambled eggs and lettuce with gelatin.

When he next left the room, He rounded on Lei. "You *are* the limit! You must have told him what you fancied."

"I never did!" protested Lei, his cheeks burning. "Not after what Old Lu told us. . . ."

Just then their host came back with a large pot of gruel — the same gruel that they had eaten the previous day. Neither young worker made any comment, but each was puzzled.

The three of them started their meal. The young peasant set a heaped bowl of rice before Lei, saying, "I know what you like."

"Anything goes for me," Lei made haste to assure him.

He shot him an accusing glance but Lei, very injured, refused to meet his eyes.

They started chatting. And their host, helping them to gruel, remarked, "This is barley kernel gruel. It's made from the green kernels of freshly reaped barley. We have a saying in these parts that mid-June is the time for three treats: fresh garlic, young lettuce and new barley. These kernels come from newly ripened barley and in the old days we wouldn't have dreamed of eating them. But we had a good crop this year, and we'd sown some in our private plot. So we'd like to treat you to this now you're here."

As the meal proceeded, both He and Lei had the feeling that the young peasant was no stranger.

They talked about the power plant and foreman Lu.

"Foreman Lu has eaten here too," their host informed them. "He's a fine man. Our villagers say that just by looking at the way Old Lu planned the power line and how to use as little arable land and materials as possible, they see the fine qualities of our brother workers."

He broke off to urge young Lei to have more gruel. But the latter had already drunk three large bowls on top of the rice and side dishes. He was incapable of eating any more.

"I've had all I can manage, comrade," he protested. "Couldn't eat another thing. I'm not being polite."

A girl's laughter sounded from behind the bamboo curtain. "Who's not being polite?" she cried. "Don't give me that talk! Yesterday you said you could eat three bowls of rice and four bowls of gruel, but today you're not keeping your word."

He and Lei recognized the clear, bell-like voice they had heard earlier on the road. Flushing and grinning, they called back: "Today's different from yesterday!"

1963

Translated by Gladys Yang

Li Zhun, Mongolian, was born in 1928 in Mengjin County, Henan Province. He began publishing short stories in 1952 and in 1954 became a member of the Henan Federation of Literary and Art Circles. Since then he has produced more than 50 short stories and novellas, film scripts and plays, most of which describe changes in rural China during the fifties and sixties.

He is now a council member of the Chinese Writers' Association.

五十年代小说选

熊 猫 丛 书

＊

《中国文学》雜志社出版

（中国北京百万庄路24号）

中国国际图书贸易总公司发行

（中国国际书店）

外文印刷厂印刷

1984年第1版

编号：（英）2—916—23

00160

10—E—1763P